THE PETTICOAT SOCIETY

Jason Prugar

PRAISE FOR JASON PRUGAR

CHASING BETTY

" **I enjoyed the hell out of this.**" - Maia Sepp, author of *The Sock Wars*

"I thoroughly enjoyed this book...kept me engaged and on the edge of my seat! I highly recommend." — Allie Frost, Author of *I'm With You*

THE PETTICOAT SOCIETY

"Jason Prugar is an immensely skilled writer...This book's interesting cast of characters fully complements a great storyline. A must read!" - Walter Stoffel, author of Lance: A Spirit Unbroken

For Those That Use Their Imagination

TALES OF GEARS & GRIT

Explore the Tales of Gears & Grit, where the brilliance of imperial treasures mask the tarnish of London's industrial grime.

Here, steampunk innovation imbues every facet of life from the glow of gas lamps to towering airships patrolling the skies.

The shared universe unfolds to the fabric of time-honored tales retold with a twist. Each installment offers a self-contained journey, yet subtle threads interweave, connecting characters, inventions and intrigues.

Embark on journey where the clash of gears echo the pulse of history and where each adventure offers a glimpse into a world where the grit of everyday life meets the grandeur of steampunk fantasy.

CHAPTER 1

"This isn't what I meant by reaching new heights," Inspector Nigel Barrington muttered as he hung from the window ledge. Sweat trickled down his face, seeping into his brown eyes.

Despite poor visibility, he knew a fatal fall awaited beneath the thick London fog. The figure to his left concerned him more than anything else on the ledge. A man in a leather jacket with wing-like sleeves, fuel-propelled boots, and a mask with eye and mouth openings.

He was the infamous, elusive Spring-Heeled Jack, and Nigel caught him. The menace terrorized the city for the past month by scaring the citizens and causing damage to homes. Nigel, a police inspector, had worked tirelessly to bring this creature to justice. Currently, the felon sat unconscious, fastened to pipes by a magnetized pair of handcuffs.

Nigel felt more water hit his face. "My word, am I really perspiring so?" He wanted to wipe it away but didn't dare make his ascent more treacherous.

He looked at his quarry, whose head sat bowed, motionless. Nigel didn't hear him breathing, nor see any emanate from the mask, but kept a peripheral eye on his catch nonetheless. Closing his eyes and taking a deep breath, Nigel relaxed his muscles. A cramp at this stage could prove fatal. He opened his eyes, focusing on the ledge and where he'd climb. In different circumstances, he could appreciate the artistry of the architecture of this modern office building, given his late father's profession. Instead, his hands moved across the London Clay of the building for purchase.

Grateful for his wife's insistence that he wear boots, the pointed end of Nigel's footwear gave him a foothold on the building, enough to pull himself up. His biceps and shoulder muscles screamed, threatening to pop. Nigel groaned, trying to keep it quiet as he pulled himself up onto the ledge.

Spring-Heeled Jack tilted its head in Nigel's direction, causing Nigel to gasp. Reminded of his current predicament, he strained to climb. Nigel's muscles twitched, the cool London Air not helping.

He forgot the pain in his muscles as his quarry jerked its body, trying to pull free from its makeshift prison. Nigel pushed with everything he had, getting his torso up over the ledge. He lifted his wiry leg and rolled over next to the prisoner.

Jack observed Nigel, then shifted his gaze to the sky. A low growl filled the air, and Nigel felt a vibration at his feet. His lower extremities, cooler just a minute ago, were heating. He felt like he was standing by a fireplace. His eyes grew wide with realization.

"Think you're going to bugger off on me?"

The flames of the Jack's rocket boots roared to life. The contraption holding him in place rattled, but didn't budge. Nigel gave a silent prayer of thanks that this building was a place of business and not a domicile. Things might get ugly with onlookers about.

Nigel stood as close to the rockets as he dared. He no doubt expected a ruffian like Spring-Heeled Jack to lift his leg and set Nigel ablaze should he venture too close. *Bet this hooligan has yet to meet the likes of me.*

Nigel flipped his topcoat open, revealing a belt over his waist, much like the famed gunslingers of the American West. The belt consisted of ten small holes, five on each side of the wearer's waist. Running fingers over them, Nigel at last came to a cylindrical brass rod and pulled it out. He twisted to the end, and the rod expanded from its six-inch length to thrice that size. Taking a small step backward, Nigel bent his knees and slid the rod onto the ledge.

The Spring-Heeled Jack increased the intensity of his rockets. To Nigel's surprise, the contraption – he named it the rat trap - continued to bind the perpetrator, but the pipes on the building were giving way. Nigel glided the rod over the ground faster and angled it so that it would spark.

Nigel had expected his opponent's gaze towards the action. Sparks flew towards the rockets on the back of the Spring-Heeled Jack's feet, enough to make him move away from them.

The rod vibrated slightly in Nigel's hand. Keeping his eyes on Spring-Heeled Jack, he smiled. Jack, unsure, stared at the Inspector, then attempted a headbutt. Nigel stepped back, fell to one knee, and jammed the rod against his would-be assailant's ribcage. Spring-Heeled Jack's head hit the wall and spasmed, his rockets shut down and the body went limp. Nigel caught him and guided it down on the ledge.

The Inspector held his breath to the count of three before collapsing onto the ledge, drinking in the stale air. His heart, pounding what seemed like a thousand beats per minute, took achingly long to settle down. Nigel turned onto his back, gazing at the stars above. They were difficult to see, the smoke from the chimneys not offering much of a view, but each one Nigel did glimpse was brighter than a diamond.

He turned his attention over to Spring-Heeled Jack, limp against the building. The pipe held him, but already came undone at the seam near the roof. Nigel got him just in time. In the end, it didn't matter because he caught him.

"Eureka!" He shouted, his cry echoing for miles. Normally, Nigel preferred his actions to speak for him. *When one achieves a goal, a little celebration is not an issue.*

"Oy!" a voice bellowed. Nigel looked around, but didn't see anyone outside, nor any windows open. The voice called out again. It came from the ground. Nigel looked down. The fog was still as thick as his sister's soup, so he couldn't see anyone. A lantern's light cut through the fog.

"Hello down there," Nigel said, hoping he wasn't raising his voice too high. "Look up, chaps."

"That you, Barrington?" A gruff, higher-pitched voice asked. Nigel smiled.

"Indeed, Reginald."

"What, in the name of the Queen, are you doing up there?"

"If you'd be so kind to find the proprietor of this establishment, and have him unlock the door, I'd be happy to show you."

***

Spring-Heeled Jack was about a head shorter than Nigel, who stood out at almost two meters tall. But whatever he had on under his clothes weighed considerably more than Nigel thought. But there was no way on God's green earth that he was getting any help in carrying Jack out. Nigel found it wise to have two colleagues in the front and back, in case the burden became overwhelming. No sense in damaging the prospects of conviction because of an injury, or worse, death.

Outside, Reginald Coates waited, leaning against the police carriage that he traveled in. Twirling his mustache, he chuckled when he saw Nigel walking out.

"I never expected to see the day when you would actually contribute your fair share of work as a police officer."

"At long last, I caught him," Nigel said, motioning for Reginald to move aside. He did, his eyes not moving off Spring-Heeled Jack. Nigel lowered the criminal into the carriage, yet he still bumped Jack's head on the floor.

Nigel winced, but Reginald just shrugged. "Although he doesn't resemble the Menace of Manchester, his helmet assures your safety."

Nigel just shook his head. "I can count on you for humor."

Reginald groaned while getting into the driver's seat. His friend gained weight and as a result, became slower with each passing season. "My darling wife is a right marvelous cook," Reginald said, more than once.

Nigel smiled and climbed into the carriage as Reginald got the horses moving. He steadied himself against the seat as the carriage wobbled on the uneven cobblestone road.

Deep down, he was worried about his friend. Reginald seemed overwhelmed by job pressures he wouldn't acknowledge. Nigel brought up the possibility of desk work, but Reginald would shut it down. It might be time to approach the subject again, this time with greater sensitivity. That could wait, however. It was time to explore the mysterious fugitive in the cab below. At the next stop, Nigel went into the cab.

Nigel studied Spring-Heeled Jack's outfit, trying to get a sense of how it all worked. "This is something Charles would love. Perhaps I can somehow let him take a look at it."

Right now, though, his priority remained the rockets. Right now, though, his focus remained on the rockets as he strapped them to his boots, much like his "tool" belt. Nigel attempted to unstrap it, but upon touching it, realized it was metal and not leather, despite its appearance. "Either that's a new metal I'm not privy to, or that's one dandy of a paint job," he muttered aloud.

The metal was warm, not too hot. It occurred to Nigel that leather would be a poor choice for the rocket, but the metal would have to stand up to the high temperatures the rockets would emit. He made a mental note as he undid them to delve deeper into that. For now, he got the rockets off.

Reginald tapped on the hood. "We're here," he said. Nigel adjusted his coat and hat. He tried to keep his smile in check, but he couldn't. When Reginald opened the door, the toothy grin on Jack's mask caused the Bobbie to shake his head. "Get a move on. I want this circus to be over. I need a proper night's rest."

CHAPTER 2

The Lehman Street police station was the dapper gentleman amongst the common, unwashed masses around it. The clean brick, spotless windowpane, and blue light above the door serve as a beacon to those in need.

For Nigel, tonight would be the start of his notoriety, and he hoped, a steppingstone on his ascent to Scotland Yard. He once again turned down Reginald's offer of assistance, lifting Spring-Heeled Jack and hoisting him over his shoulder. The lack of the rockets lightened Nigel's load a hair, but walking into the precinct with his quarry made him feel weightless.

The shop to the station's right was closing, its owner locking up. Nigel heard the key bounce off the road, and he smiled. Murmurs and whispers filled the air like a sudden gust of wind in the chilly London air. Nigel smiled, taking it all in. Adjusting his long strides to measured beats, he enabled more people to witness what he had. Even the small twinge in his back did little to temper his enthusiasm.

Nigel pushed the door hard enough that people inside would hear him. Sure enough, his fellow constables, as well as the riffraff inside, turned their attention to him.

"I say, is there a magister present?"

"What the bloody hell do you have there, Barrington?" Chief Inspector Willoughby asked. The man, in his late fifties but strong like someone ten years younger, watched Nigel with hands on hips.

"Follow me, and I'll show you."

Willoughby looked at Reginald. "We have a lot of serious activity this evening, Barrington. This had better not be a frivolity."

Nigel approached the cells and nodded to the constable, a fresh-faced young man, his uniform clean, his badge shiny. *Must be his first week.* The youth fumbled with the keys, dropping them twice, the door clanking open on the third try.

Nigel entered and, as carefully as he could manage, laid Spring-Heeled Jack in the cell. He stepped aside to allow the Chief to enter. Several inspectors and bobbies came over. If Willoughby became interested in something, it was worth their interest as well.

The Chief Inspector stepped closer, eyeing Spring-Heeled Jack, stroking his beard as he took in the garish costume. "That looks like one of the bit players from the Old Vic!" Willoughby said.

"Chief," Nigel interjected. "Not Shakespeare, but still imaginative. This..." Nigel paused. Though not a storyteller or showman, this was his moment, and he felt it deserved a touch of flair. "...is Spring-Heeled Jack."

Willoughby's breath came in short huffs. He shifted his weight, putting his hands back on his hips, his face reddening.

"*This* is your infamous Spring-Heeled Jack? It appears to be from a costume party! You had me devote resources and time to *this*?"

"In fairness, sir, *I* was the only one pursuing this case."

"To the detriment of other, standard police work. We have two families out front asking for help in finding their missing daughters! A case *you* asked to pursue after the death of the first one!"

"You gave me authority to chase leads, sir," Nigel said. "While not responsible for the missing girls, this individual may have ties to the case. And the only extraneous resources expended were among my personal items."

"Which almost caused a scandal, in front of the local magistrate," Willoughby retorted. "I thought you said this beast was a devil? That he could fly? I don't see wings. The mask doesn't resemble a devil's face. Why, it barely has horns!"

Nigel exhaled and pulled Jack's arms outward and Jack's wings opened, which led to nervous murmurs in the room.

"He utilizes small cylinders that combine steam and petroleum to form a combustion reaction to propel him to flight," Nigel said. Willoughby stared at him.

Reginald leaned in to his superior. "He's talking about rockets, sir. I've seen them. They're being brought in for evidence."

"And the mask lights up. I have yet to discover the mechanism that provides it," Nigel said. "But I would think if you saw this leaping over a wall at all hours of the night, with its eye sockets lit up, you'd consider it devilish."

"If the magister doesn't agree with you, Barrington," Willoughby said, "You'll find yourself sidelined. There are young girls missing. Now, let's discover who this unfortunate soul is, lest he stake a claim of cruelty against us."

Deflated, Nigel knelt next to the prisoner, studying the mask. It didn't appear to slide on the head. He ran a finger over it, the brass surface relatively smooth. *Not accustomed to hitting his head. A rather skillful chap.* Near the horns, Nigel's fingertip felt a ridge. He followed it with his eyes. He tried prying it off, but all he did was jerk the head.

"For Heaven's sake, man, be careful!" Willoughby chided.

Nigel tapped his chin with his finger, the pose which he used since boyhood whenever deep in thought. Unlike his brother Charles, he wasn't a prodigy, but he wasn't a simpleton either. He had to concentrate more.

Nigel ran his fingers over the ridge, tracing the small front horns. He tapped them and tried to pull, but nothing. The ridges went through them.

"I've tried everything," he mumbled. "It has to be here."

Then it hit him: he *didn't* try everything. Nigel twisted the horns, and they turned. The mask whirred and made a grinding noise. It hissed as steam escaped. The mask fell off in two pieces, and the Chief caught them.

"My word," Willoughby exhaled.

The man seated there was hardly an adult. If Nigel had to guess, he'd say the chap had recently completed his second decade of life.

But he didn't have to guess. He knew the man, whose youthful visage graced paintings throughout the commonwealth as a muse of local artists. Despite his envious looks, he had a birthmark above his left eyebrow. Nigel knew that the youth was very rich, but didn't flaunt it, either in hairstyle or dress. He was a credit to his class, that of a noble.

"Lord Ainsworth," Willoughby and Nigel muttered.

Lord Hannibal Ainsworth turned 21 and, since his brother, Percival, had married, was eligible to wed. Many a maiden had wondered aloud if they'd be the lucky bride, including Nigel's sister, Minnie, who just stepped out into British society herself.

His mouth sat agape. Ainsworth was a mere youth, going to balls to look for a wife and expand his family's fortunes. What motivated him to endanger everything by terrorizing the people? Nigel couldn't fathom an answer as he scratched the part of his head that stuck out under his hat.

Upon his name departing Willoughby's lips, the young noble stirred, moaning and rubbing his temple. He looked up, blinking his green eyes to adjust to the light.

"My lord, I am Chief Inspector Willoughby. I am terribly sorry about this misunderstanding." He turned to Reginald. "Get this man a chair."

Reginald nodded and went to get one. "A comfortable one, Reginald. Bring the one from my office."

Nigel's hands shook as Willoughby continued to pamper the young aristocrat. Feelings of confusion and betrayal gnawed at Nigel's conscience. His fingers, often steady and sure, now trembled as they traced the outline of his desk, seeking purchase in a world spun upside down. His brow furrowed as he remembered the terrified Londoners, knowing it wasn't a common criminal, but a privileged man responsible for their misery. A man who treated lives as mere playthings. And why? Because he *could?*

"Can you stand, my lord?" He asked, offering his hand to Ainsworth.

"I believe so," Ainsworth replied. He took Willoughby's hand and stood, groaning as he got upright. Ainsworth nodded his thanks and stretched out.

"My lord, I cannot apologize enough for this very unfortunate misunderstanding. My men, while passionate in their diligence, sometime overstep their bounds, as Inspector Barrington did this night."

Nigel's hand balled into fists, and he put his arms behind his back, taking a deep breath to calm himself. He glanced at the door and observed his colleagues, who were gathered there, swiftly dispersing and feigning busyness.

"I beg your pardon my lord, but Chief Inspector, that isn't--"

"I promise you that a full investigation into this unfortunate event will be conducted and -- "

"Now sir," Nigel said.

"Inspector, you will keep quiet! I-"

"Barrington wasn't wrong, Chief Inspector," Ainsworth said, causing both inspectors' jaws to drop. "The Spring-Heeled Jack is real, and I am he."

CHAPTER 3

Lord Ainsworth sat straight and still in Willoughby's chair, which Nigel moved back to the Chief Inspector's office. A local magistrate, whose night clothes peeked out of his topcoat, made it in. *Naturally, one could be summoned when a noble was involved.*

Willoughby provided the magistrate with a glass of water. Ainsworth took a glass as well, though his requested whiskey lapped its edges. Nigel's stomach roiled at the Chief Inspector's deference to the aristocrat, whom, other than his status as an eligible bachelor, had little else going for him. But Willoughby knew who could help keep him in his post, and he played to that.

The magister, now lucid enough to do his job, was writing notes. He motioned for Ainsworth to continue.

"I am aware of the attacks on young women, some debutantes and some of them amongst the common people," Ainsworth said, not looking up at the coppers.

"I've been privy to some talk amongst the men in my class, that they've experienced peculiar sightings. At first, they attributed it to excitement after an evening of frivolity. Then, two of them experienced these sightings on their property. Imagine my surprise when they said they had beaks of birds in human form."

"That *is* a surprise," Willoughby added.

"One of them scared the sister of a dear friend, and I felt I had to act. She said she saw a demon. So I used my resources to craft a visage of fear, to strike terror into *their* hearts."

"I never meant to harm anyone. And I don't think you can blame me for a woman given to hysterics. I stuck to less populated areas. At least not when they are likely to be out."

Nigel felt his face flush, and he pulled out his notebook, his hands shaking in anger, which made it difficult to rifle through pages. "Actually, my lord, --"

Willoughby cleared his throat, staring daggers at Nigel.

Nigel squeezed his notebook tight, his nails digging into the leather cover.

"It's quite all right, Chief Inspector," Ainsworth continued. "I want to clarify that I had nothing to do with that poor girl's death."

"She didn't die, my lord," Willoughby said. "She fainted like someone about to go before God, but she lived."

Nigel studied Ainsworth's reaction. His posture relaxed, his eyelid closed to a normal size. Nigel rifled through his notebook, scanning an entry from three days prior.

"You didn't stay long enough to see that woman go down the other night. No, you're talking about the death in Camden Town, three weeks ago. *You were there.*"

Willoughby turned red, his old cockney accent coming to the fore, making his words impossible to understand. The magister tried talking over him, then to Nigel, but he couldn't talk loud enough. Nigel closed his eyes, steadying himself. His lips pressed into a thin line to stifle the words of protest that threatened to spill forth unbidden.

"Oy!" Reginald yelled, standing in the hallway. Everyone looked at him. "My apologies, sir."

Nigel turned back to Ainsworth. "So you admit you were there, at the site of the murder?"

"I didn't arrive until after she was dead," Ainsworth said. "My mask can see body heat."

"Really? Fascinating."

"Yes, and the heat was all gone." Ainsworth leaned forward, making sure everyone could hear. "There is something going on. It's big-"

"Chief Inspector," a new, deeper voice said from the hallway behind the office, "I hope you're not eager to try your luck against Ainsworth at chess. He's a notorious hustler."

Nigel and Willoughby spun around to see a sartorially superior gentleman standing there, leaning on a walking cane. Bowler tipped forward, his kept beard trimmed as neat as possible. Mirth danced in his green eyes, but his smile betrayed less than proper intentions.

"Lord Rushforth!" Willoughby said, standing to shake the newcomer's hand. "What a pleasure. How may I help you?"

"I'm wondering if I could talk to you in private?"

Willoughby nodded, allowed Rushforth to exit. He gave Nigel a curt nod, but his eyes were now ice. He kept his gaze on Rushforth until the noble left the room.

"Can we continue this?"

"I prefer the Chief Inspector here," the magister said, stifling a yawn.

"I'm the arresting inspector. Is my word and presence not enough?"

The magister tapped his quill on the side of the inkwell. "I suppose we can gather the rest of his personal information."

As the magister started talking, Nigel exhaled and tuned him out, leaning back in his chair as Willoughby's hearty laugh filled the air. Nigel turned his ear toward the glass, hoping to hear a snippet of their conversation, but just got muffled sounds.

Nigel reached into his pocket and pulled out a small piece of tube, about four inches long. On one end was a cone, like a funnel. The other resembled a reed from an oboe, an instrument his mother used to play. He twisted it into an *S* shape. Nigel put the tube in his left hand. Leaning back in his chair, he rested his head against his left hand, and put the bent tube around his ear, the cone facing the glass.

The sound improved in clarity, but still remained too muffled. Nigel used his thumb and forefinger to twist the cone. This time, he caught a stray word that Rushforth and Willoughby said, but nothing that raised suspicion. More small-talk about the police bootlicking the upper crust.

The magistrate cleared this throat within a couple of feet of Nigel's face. "I say, is that satisfactory?"

"You've gathered all of his information, but you will not ask more questions?"

"Not without the Chief Inspector."

Nigel sighed. "Fine."

Willoughby entered the room, his laughter subsiding as he walked in. "That will be all for tonight, gentlemen. Lord Ainsworth, you're free to go."

"I beg your pardon, sir?" Nigel asked.

"I believe I was quite clear, Nigel. You will escort Lord Ainsworth outside."

"But-"

"Another word, and you are suspended."

Nigel's hands shook, and he felt his face get flush. "Right away, sir."

Lord Ainsworth stood up, adjusting his coat and standing up straight. "Thank you, Chief Inspector. I apologize for any inconvenience that I may have caused."

"Not to worry, my lord." Willoughby removed his cap. "You have a pleasant evening."

Ainsworth nodded as he walked out. Nigel followed him toward the entrance. Rushforth leaned against the wall, nodding to Ainsworth. "My carriage will take you home, milord. My man has already procured your belongings."

"Thank you."

Rushforth turned his attention to Nigel, straightening himself. He wasn't as tall as the inspector, but his presence, his gaze, put Nigel on edge. But he stayed rigid, not backing down. "Lord Rushforth."

"Inspector Burnham-"

"It's Barrington."

"That's the issue with inspectors," Rushforth said. "Always focusing on the minor details, unable to see things from above."

"It is my job to deal with the facts," Nigel said, "And when I don't have them, find them."

"I'm always amused at people who can't see what is right in front of them."

"If I'm missing something," Nigel retorted, "I'd be appreciative to learn what it is."

"One thing my father taught me is that growth comes from doing things yourself," Rushforth said, smiling. "It would be improper of me to rob you of that privilege."

"I take pride in solving a case," Nigel said. "Finding all the pieces of the puzzle. I look forward to finding the missing ones here."

Nigel leaned in toward Rushforth. "No matter who holds them."

Rushforth smiled. "Good evening, Inspector. It's a dangerous city. Stay on guard."

CHAPTER 4

"Sir, how can you just let him go?"

"Lord Rushforth is one of our most important patrons, donating to the Police Assistance Fund since he took over his family estate. He asked it as a personal favor, which he plans to repay at our next benefit gala."

"He all but admitted to witnessing a crime! We'd be negligent in not following this course of action."

"You will obey orders given to you by your superior officer!"

"Then order me to continue this investigation."

"Very well, inspector. You will investigate the alleged sightings of what Lord Ainsworth referred to as demons. You will start post haste."

Willoughby eyed his subordinate. "You've got passion and instincts, Nigel. But your discipline is lacking. The eyes of the nation, *and the crown*, are upon us."

"And what will they think of us if we don't solve this?"

"We *will* solve it and bring the perpetrators to justice. But we will do this the right way. For now, you will stick to your assignment and let nothing stand in the way of completing these tasks. Is that clear? Nigel calmed his breathing. "Will that be all?"

Willoughby nodded. Nigel left.

Nigel stalked away from the police building as fast as his legs would take him.

How could the Chief allow the top suspect to walk away? Lord Ainsworth was on the low rung on the ladder, Rushforth not much higher. They could call upon a noble of their own.

Nigel noticed a carriage heading towards him, as the rapid *clop-clop* of horses' hooves echoed down the street. He stepped aside so it could pass. He chanced a look back at the building. "Let nothing stand in my way of completing my tasks, eh? Message received, sir."

Nigel stopped before his front door, admiring the exterior of his home. In the middle of a row of identical domiciles, it was one of the best-looking homes in an inspector's price range. Dubbed by the builder as modern style at ancient prices, Nigel still chuckled at the description: the *classical portico against a rogue gothic brick façade.*

Above the bay window, half of a German gothic turret roof covered the front door. Candlelight flickered in there. Nigel smiled and wasted no time walking inside.

He used a bit more force than needed closing the door, but any sound he made got drowned out by a robust, yet high-pitched laugh. "Oh, Minnie!"

Minnie Barrington came downstairs, carrying a candle and giggling. Standing about a foot shorter than her brother, her shoulder-length blonde curls bobbed as she walked. She held her white nightgown as she walked. A surge of joy filled Nigel's being as he witnessed his vivacious sister, now entering the world of debutantes, exuding an infectious energy and zest for life. *She'll settle on a single suitor soon. Which is good, because I am too busy to keep tabs on all the men chasing her.*

Their brother, Charles, came down behind her. He toyed with the goggles atop his head, wild hair growing in all directions. The middle child, Charles always had a penchant for making his siblings laugh.

This time, however, Nigel could only shake his head. Charles leapt off the bottom step, his lab coat flailing as he did so. Nigel saw that under his coat, Charles had britches on, and nothing else.

"Look who came home," Minnie said. "Good thing I sent my paramour away early."

"A long night on the job. And there is no way you're jeopardizing anything right after your society debut."

"Perish the thought," Minnie said, smiling, and giving him a smile. Charles nudged her aside and stood in front of Nigel, arms crossed.

"And you, dear brother," Nigel said, clasping Charles' shoulders. "Success?"

"Sure did. The ruffian's rocket boosters provided tremendous strain, but it held. Well done."

"Eureka!" Charles exclaimed, stepping away from his brother, clapping and high-stepping into a jig. Nigel and Minnie shared a laugh.

Charles stopped, taking a moment to catch his breath. "New notions. Come see."

"I'd love nothing more," Nigel said. "But it's been a long day. And you ought to get your rest as well. Even Charles Babbage slept."

"He did?" Charles moved up the stairs. Near the top, he stopped and spun around, arching an eyebrow at him. "Wait, *I* am Charles Babbage!"

Nigel tried not to shake his head. "Good night, dear brother."

Minnie touched his arm as he reached the top of the stairs. "You do well with him. Mom and Dad would be proud."

"*We* do well with him, dear sister. You'll make a fine mother some-day." He looked her in the eyes. He saw a lot of joy and love in there. The man who got to look at them every day would be lucky indeed.

"That assumes we don't perish in an all-consuming fire. I don't like the noises I hear in his lab."

"You have nothing to fear, dear sister. I inspect it every night. He's quite talented, a man of genius. It's a shame that while his eccentric-ities free him from constraints of societal convention, they keep him confined to our home."

"It's small minded, if you ask me," Minnie replied, her lip quiver-ing. "They don't wish to benefit from his genius because he can't hold a conversation about tea or India. Yet he can take their broken metal and craft a useful device out of it in his sleep."

"I've sometimes asked God why, dear sister. Then I remembered He works in mysterious ways," Nigel said, but it didn't stop the tears from dripping down Minnie's cheek. "Ours is not to understand."

"On that, brother, I agree, because I do *not* understand." She wiped the tears away. "You ought to get to bed. You have a big day tomorrow."

"I will, after I do my nightly check of the lab."

Minnie nodded as she ascended the stairs. Nigel stepped over to the base of the stairs. A small horse statue, its front legs in the air, rested atop the banister. He pulled it towards him. At the base of the banister, the grinding and creaking of gears filled Nigel's ears, albeit muffled. He felt the vibrations in his feet and took a step back. The banister, and the piece of the wooden floor it rested on, lifted six inches in the air. At the same time, the bottom step opened towards him. It revealed a staircase going into darkness. Nigel activated the wall lantern and descended.

Automated lanterns activated with every two steps Nigel took down the stairs. Charles said it could detect weight, which got a joke from Minnie about his 'girth'. It was all in good fun. Ivy, Nigel's wife, had uncovered early on the affection that Minnie had for Nigel. He thanked his lucky stars every day that she still saw him as a brother and not as a stern caregiver.

Not yet. Wait until the suitors come in full force.

Charles had not yet activated an automatic lantern at the base of his lab to illuminate the room, but he *was* smart enough to put the activation switch underneath the lantern above the last step. Nigel took the grip and pulled the lever down. The lanterns on the ceiling lit up, one by one, starting from the left, right over Nigel's head, to the other side of the staircase. Nigel smiled as the lanterns formed the shape of a nautilus.

Two tables that could feed a large family sat at the fore of the lab. A variety of items, including beakers, burners and a microscope, adorned them. Behind the tables was a small desk, a dozen notebooks on either side. An open notebook disclosed a sketch and Charles' illegible scribblings. Nigel turned his attention to the shelves behind the wall. There was enough space to fill it with half the books from Oxford. These shelves contained a variety of gadgets and devices, all in various stages of disrepair. Many had a knob missing here, a gear there.

Nigel touched some of them. They were rather clean, despite their age. If you didn't look too closely, they could go into a storefront tomorrow.

"I am befuddled at your apparent inability to keep your room this clean," Nigel said as he turned the light off and headed upstairs.

***

Nigel woke to the sound of laughter once again. This time the bird-like melody came from two women. Nigel sat up and opened the shutters to a bright yellow sun, its rays filling his room with beams of joy.

His finest suit hung on the back of his door, cleaned and pressed. Nigel walked over, admiring it. Every crease was crisp, no hair or lint or any foreign objects.

"I'll look like the Crown Prince," Nigel muttered. He grabbed his robe from the edge of the bed and sauntered downstairs.

Nigel followed the polite chat and laughter into the kitchen, where Charles, thankfully clothed, sat next to Minnie and across from another woman. Charles looked at Nigel and said, "The head of the pride awakens from thine slumber!"

The woman turned and stood. Her rose-red lips parted into a smile, her green eyes bright light diamonds. She wore a form fitting dress of emerald, her corset accentuating her curves, down to her billowing hoop shirt.

"Ivy," he said.

"Good morning, dear," Ivy said, looking up with wide yet devilish grin on her face. She was thinking certain marital thoughts.

My darling wife. The sun that penetrates the darkness. How did I get so lucky?

"My beloved, while that sounds fetching, what will that teach Minnie? She might try to do that with every suitor who comes calling."

"If they are all as magnificent as you, Nigel, I should think you'd want that."

"On the contrary. I want her to have the opposite of me. Because I know the thoughts that pop into my head when you appear, and they do more than make my heart flutter."

Ivy gasped in mocked indignation, then slapped his hand. "Naughty! I suggest you don't say that around my father. He tries to portray us as members of polite society."

"He might be happy to hear that Inspector Barrington single-handedly nabbed the Spring-Heeled Jack last night."

"Really?"

"It was as much a tribute to my brother's genius as to my training, but yes."

"I'm so proud," Ivy said. "I believe we should lead with that tonight."

"What we *should* lead with is his favorite drink and some food. Speaking of which," Nigel said, looking at Minnie, "Are we all set?"

"The carriage will be here within the hour," Minnie replied. "So hurry about and get dressed. They can't see you looking like that."

"Quite right, Minnie," Ivy added.

"Afraid they'll get the wrong idea?"

Ivy tossed her fan at him as he ran upstairs.

Minnie's room was across the hall from Ivy and Nigel's. It was decorated about the same: canopy bed, changing screen, a wardrobe and dresser were all that adorned the space. Atop the dresser laid a pink mirror, the object of Nigel's hunt.

Nigel slowly entered his sister's bedroom, each step calculated. The floor upstairs was creaking more than normal, something on his to-do list – provided he would ever again have enough time off to attend to such duties. Right now, they were playing along as he inched closer to his goal.

He reached for the mirror's handle hanging off the edge of the dresser and took another step.

Creak.

"Of course," he whispered. He grabbed the mirror.

"You could've just asked."

Startled, Nigel stumbled and fell to one knee, almost dropping the mirror. He looked up to see Minnie standing there, arms crossed, trying not to laugh.

"I'd apologize for startling you, but such endeavors yield rich rewards."

"I'm glad I amuse you. And what would walking around with this mirror do for my image as an upstanding member of Her Majesty's Police Force?"

"Add to your delusions of grandeur," Minnie said. "Ivy asked if you would stop by the bakery and pick up the cakes on the way over. They are her father's favorite."

"As soon as I make myself presentable. Thank you."

"Make sure you use the mirror first."

***

The morning air was colder than Nigel expected, and he cursed himself for not letting his hair dry before coming outside. Or at least not choosing a warmer hat.

Nigel used the crisp air, and fear of chills, to speed his walk to the bakery. He'd balked at this kind of activity more than once, but since Ivy planned everything else for the brunch, and didn't object to his long hours, he felt it was the least he could do.

The bakery business was as brisk as the cool, English air. The bells on the door jingled at a steady pace as patrons moved in and out. Nigel grabbed the door handle, opening it in time for a mother and son to exit, each carrying a small box.

A young man stood in front of him in line dressed in a fine suit. An older man stood by him. Nigel guessed he was in his fifties. The older gentleman had a suit on, but of lesser quality, fraying at the wrist and collar. It surprised Nigel to see Lord Ainsworth standing there when the younger man turned to talk. He stepped forward, leaning closer to the young noble.

"If a man of your stature is here," Nigel said, "Then I made the right choice in baked goods."

Ainsworth and his friend turned around. The man wore a sneer along with his old suit. His right eye was permanently in a squint and the wrinkles on his face made him seem old.

"Inspector, fancy meeting you here." He motioned to the man. "This is my majordomo, Lester."

"Nigel Barrington." He offered a hand, which Lester took. His grip was stronger than Nigel expected.

"My grandmother, God rest her soul, used to bring me bread from this place. I stop by whenever I am around," Ainsworth said, leaning in. "I try not to take *too* much advantage of my station, but I find a personal appearance assures me of at least one fresh loaf."

"Is this a regular occurrence?"

"Not nearly enough," Ainsworth mused.

"Is that because you're investigating those demons of yours?"

"Oy," Lester said, stepping between them. "I unfastened ye superior warned ye of such talk. Might file a wee report on my lord's behalf a'gin you."

Nigel stared into the man's good eye, then at Ainsworth. The young man looked like he wanted to talk, but something held him back.

"My apologies, Lord Ainsworth. I'm sorry if I upset you. Good day."

Ainsworth took his order and left. Nigel's was waiting when he got to the front, making his stay after the confrontation short.

***

Nigel took a moment to place the cakes in a small blue box, which Ivy said was her father's favorite color. *I need all the good tidings I can get.*

He replayed reacting to Ainsworth and his man at the bakery. It was odd that a young aristocrat would be there, but Nigel felt it was Providence. But the exchange frustrated him. Being an inspector allowed him to pursue his curiosity in the course of his work. But now with the strict parameters imposed on him, coupled with Ainsworth being untouchable, he had to leave.

His frustration was gone – mostly – by the time he stepped in the living room in time to see Ivy come down the stairs, and Nigel almost tripped over himself. She wore a dark purple dress, with matching corset and gloves. Swirling black embroidery adorned the hoop skirt. She topped it off with a matching hat.

"Never has something so lovely passed in front of these eyes," Nigel said.

Ivy stopped, eyeing her husband and took a long look before planting a firm, loving kiss on his lips. "You are too good to me, love. I must look the part of the wife of London's brightest young inspector."

"You look like the most beautiful woman in the world."

Minnie broke this line of talk up by coughing. "That worked for you?" She asked Ivy.

"No," she replied, patting Nigel's hand when he opened his mouth to intervene. "It just confirms I made the right choice."

"I only like sap on my breakfast cakes, thank you."

"More for Ivy and me. Right, dear?"

"Indeed. When the right man comes, Minnie, you'll change your mind."

"Time will tell. Speaking of time, if we don't take the coach now, we'll be late."

"Charles?" Nigel asked, and Minnie pointed to the floor. "Oh no. I told him. Not today."

Nigel activated the lever and went down the stairs as quickly as he could, not worrying about scuffing his shoes or falling. At the bottom of the stairs, he saw Charles sitting on the bench, his back toward Nigel.

"Brother, we've gone over again and again how important today is. We cannot have you down here-"

Charles turned around, revealing his work. Two brass gears, which looked brand new, sat encased in a glass dome.

"What is that?"

"Surprise, now ruined. Made for you and sister Ivy. Gears."

"I can see that."

"Alone, just parts, no purpose. Together, they are one machine."

"Thank you, Charles, it's wonderful."

"I know. Not ruin the surprise for sister Ivy? Let me give it to her?"

"Of course."

Charles shut the light down in the lab, and the two brothers walked side-by-side to the main floor.

CHAPTER 5

Mary adjusted her new red hat as she waited on the corner. Aunt Thomasine, her chaperone, waited next to her, wearing a green and black ensemble. A radiant smile spread across Mary's face as she marveled at her crisp red dress and snug corset. She had to look perfect for her date.

She wished her prospective beau could court her without her aunt there, but her father wouldn't have it. A young man - important, and to Mary's delight, rich - had asked to see her, much to her father's liking.

Mary wasn't sure why they were meeting near Camden Town. It didn't seem like an area where a man of his stature would put himself, but she chalked it up to business interests. Aunt Thomasine told her not to question it. "If a man this influential is interested, you should be thankful for his attentions. He has the resources to keep you well."

Mary sensed the tinge of not-quite-jealous hopefulness. Her late Uncle wasn't much of a husband, but he provided Thomasine with food, good clothing, and a roof over her head.

A carriage crossed in front of them and Mary took off, ignoring her aunt's pleas for patience. She heard the waddle of her aunt's shoes on the cobblestones. Thomasine had to drag her right leg to walk because of a bad knee and hip, and wouldn't be able to keep up. It was getting dark, and she wasn't sure that her potential beau would wait. Her father had insisted they walk, so Mary wouldn't get excited and risk potential embarrassment by touching, or heaven forbid, kiss. She figured it gave her aunt a chance to go over all the things a "proper young woman" did in these situations.

She turned left at the butcher shop, just as her date instructed. The alley only had one lantern, but Mary saw she was alone. Aunt Thomasine's pleas had died down, in part because Mary was getting concerned at her current state. Was she being tricked? Did she get dressed up for nothing, just a ruse to serve the crude entertainment of a class above her station?

Mary turned around, ready to go. She heard a soothing, "Hello." Mary smiled. That voice was familiar.

She turned, smiling, but ran into a handkerchief that covered her nose and mouth. Before she could utter a word or protest, her world went black.

By the time Thomasine rounded the corner, the alley was empty again.

✦

CHAPTER 6

Charles presented Ivy the gear in the carriage on their way to the party. She couldn't hold back tears, almost bringing him to tears as well. *I couldn't have asked for a better start to the party,* Nigel thought.

The Lovelace residence was one of the oldest homes about Bloomsbury. Thanks to the wealth that Ivy's father earned in the technology business, they had doubled the size of their home, making it a true Victorian mansion. Two stories high, the roof, updated within the past year, was red. It had three turrets on the second story, and a large balcony above the porch, which wrapped around the left side of the home. The right side contained a large stable, which Charles pointed out was almost as big as Nigel's house.

Ivy greeted Mortimer, the head of the house, with a hug. A rail-thin man with impeccable manners and posture, and a warm smile, Mortimer held Ivy like a favorite niece.

"It's lovely to see you, Miss Ivy," he said, his eyes widening upon realizing what he said. "My apologies, Mrs. Barrington."

"You never have to apologize. It's a lifelong habit, I'm sure."

Mortimer exhaled and smiled. "Thank you. And may I say that you look as if you belong in the Queen's court."

"Thank you."

Mortimer bowed as Nigel entered, along with his siblings, then led them inside.

"May I present Nigel and Ivy Barrington, and his siblings Charles and Minnie Barrington."

"Ivy, my child!" A woman called out.

"Hello, mother!"

A woman who looked like she could be Ivy's older sister moved across the room to hug Ivy. Mrs. Lovelace sported a conservative yet colorful blue dress, a more demure hoop skirt than Ivy's. She shared the same green eyes as Ivy. She turned those eyes to Nigel.

He offered his hand. "Mum, thank you for hosting this and welcoming us."

"Charmed, my dear," she said, enveloping him in a hug. "Now come, let's get you settled before dinner is ready."

***

Nigel offered to help, but his mother-in-law wouldn't have it. "Not only are you my guest, but Margaret and Henrietta are top flight cooks," Mrs. Lovelace said, beaming. "They'll have the entire dinner prepared before you peel a single potato."

They moved to the parlor and small talk ensued, in which Nigel dutifully partook. But something irked him. Checking his watch, he noticed it was a half hour after they were told to arrive, and he had yet to see Mr. Lovelace.

He saw Charles across the room, discussing something scientific that surprised Mortimer, given his jaw was stuck in an open position. On the other side of the room, Henrietta tended to the bread as Margaret poured something into a large bowl.

Nigel strode over to them. "Mum, I do apologize, but may I borrow my bride?"

He walked her toward the foyer. "Your father's not here."

"I'd wager he's conducting business in the study."

"But a half hour late to his own dinner?"

Ivy's smile faded.

"There's my lovely daughter!" a soft, yet powerful baritone said behind them. Nigel whipped around.

An older man stood there, smiling as he looked at Ivy. His gray muttonchops were well groomed and he leaned against a cane. His top hat barely reached Nigel's forehead. His pinstripe suit was older but better tailored than the other guests.

Nigel's bride walked over and took the hat from him. "Hello, father!"

Standing patiently, Nigel motioned to Minnie, pointing to the kitchen. She shrugged her shoulders. Nigel rolled his eyes, mouthing the word, "box". Minnie nodded and disappeared.

Lovelace turned his steel-blue eyes to Nigel. The man may not have been a titan in terms of height, but everyone there could feel his presence. He moved in a calculated manner toward Nigel, who knew the entire place had gone silent. Was gossip really such an issue in this town? *I'll have to check with Ivy on that later. Or maybe Minnie.*

Nigel offered his hand. "Good evening, sir. It's an honor to dine with you in your home."

"The honor is mine, Nigel."

Minnie appeared behind Mr. Lovelace, holding the box aloft so Nigel would see it. "I have something for you."

Mr. Lovelace raised an eyebrow, watching Nigel take the box from Minnie. Nigel held it in front of his father-in-law. "I understand you have a fondness for these."

Mr. Lovelace removed the bow and opened the box, revealing a dozen small chocolate cakes. His expression hardly changed, though his eyes widened a hair. If Nigel wasn't looking at him, or trained as a detective, he would've missed it. Mr. Lovelace nodded to the box, and Nigel gestured for him to indulge.

Mr. Lovelace grabbed one, and took a small bite, eyeing his daughter and Nigel as he chewed. When he swallowed, he replaced the cake in the box and said, "Thank you. Those bring back the happiest memories of youth." Nigel took Lovelace's outstretched hand and shook it. He exhaled the breath he didn't realize he'd been holding in.

***

The quail, potatoes and vegetables were all cooked to perfection, which Nigel determined as soon as he took the first bite of each one.

"This meal is quite exquisite, Mum," Nigel said.

Mr. Lovelace made a noise, which Nigel heard as a huff. It was subtle, and Nigel guessed he heard it because he was two seats over from his father-in-law. If anyone else heard it, they kept that information to themselves.

"Thank you, Nigel," his mother-in-law said. "Margaret knows it's one of my husband's favorites. And Ivy loves the potato seasoning."

"I do hope you share that recipe, Mother,' Ivy said. "I want to make this."

Mr. Lovelace put this fork down, wiping the corners of his mouth with a napkin. "Your servant."

"I beg your pardon, father?"

"You mean your servant will make dinner for Nigel."

"Father, I've told you," Ivy said in a measured response. "We don't have a servant yet."

Mr. Lovelace turned to Nigel. "And why is that?"

Swallowing his quail without chewing, Nigel quickly put his napkin to mouth as he coughed. Ivy's mother made it less embarrassing by whispering something to her husband. "I felt it prudent to wait until my next appraisal, when I expect another small raise that will allow me to compensate someone fairly."

"I see," Mr. Lovelace said, sipping wine. "And tell me, does any of your recent policing activities reflect upon that appraisal?"

Nigel raised an eyebrow, as he detected a sarcastic bite to that question. "You must be talking about an inspector that leads his precinct in cases closed the past three months, or capturing the public menace known as Spring-Heeled Jack. Yes, I should think so."

Ivy beamed at this, and her mom let out a gasp of joyous surprise.

"I was referring to the situation of a man who ignores direct orders from superiors and mistakenly arrests members of the aristocracy to the point of being given a final warning before suspension."

Ivy and Minnie gasped at this. Nigel's mouth opened, but nothing came out. His heart feeling like it leapt to his throat might have had something to do with that. How did Lovelace find this out? And why choose now – at an event he and his wife hosted – to embarrass him in front of Ivy?

"Darling," Mrs. Lovelace whispered to her husband.

"I am not as versed in policing as the technology business," Mr. Lovelace continued, "But your Chief Inspector Willoughby shares drinks with me at the Ellington Club. He's rather concerned about inspectors like that."

"Lord Ainsworth admitted to being Spring-Heeled Jack," Nigel said. "He frightened women, one almost to the point of death. He had to be stopped, and he was. My instincts were correct."

"I have heard great things about you. But I have also heard you act in a manner detrimental to yourself and others."

"I get the job done, sir."

"Being on probation is not what I would call getting the job done. Nor does it give me confidence that you can provide *my only child* with the life she deserves."

"Father!" Ivy pleaded.

Nigel raised a hand. "Sir, as someone who cares and loves another," he said, looking at Ivy, "I can appreciate where you're coming from. I will not apologize for doing my job the best way I know how, nor will I ignore what I believe to be one of the most important tools I possess to do the job. The fact remains that a being who terrorized Her Majesty's Subjects is no longer on the streets."

He stood and bowed to Mrs. Lovelace. "Thank you for a lovely meal," Nigel said, and pulled out a small bottle of brandy from his interior jacket pocket. "I know this isn't your favorite brandy, sir, but I figured you might like it. Maybe more than you like me."

Nigel got up and left. Ivy's mother threw her napkin on the table. Ivy stood as well.

"I hope you're proud, father," Ivy said. "And if you didn't like him, you shouldn't have approved the wedding. For better or worse, I am his and he is mine."

She left. Minnie and Charles bowed and rushed out after them.

***

The coach ride home was silent, and went quicker than expected, because Nigel replayed the dinner over and over in his mind. Mr. Lovelace expressed no outward hostility toward him before, even during engagement negotiations. Sure, he bristled at the first mention of Nigel's profession, but his concerns ceased after Chief Willoughby had talked to him.

Nigel knew that technically, his family's station was lower than Ivy's, but his parents saved religiously, and he got a sizable inheritance when they died. That helped matters, as did the time they spent with the Lovelace family during the engagement.

Before he could complete his ruminations, they were home. Nigel helped his wife and sister out of the carriage. Once inside, he went upstairs to the bedroom.

Nigel enjoyed a good book – when he had time to read – but since their home wasn't that big, he didn't have a study. Nigel took advantage of the corner of the bedroom near a window to read. Now, he used it to think.

The night was clear, and he got a decent view of London lit up. Sure, his neighbor's home partially obscured this view, but it gave him a focal point for his thoughts.

Thankfully, divorce wasn't an option. It took an act of Parliament to grant a divorce and even that was rare, and to date, only for the aristocracy, who needed it as to cut their financial losses. Marriage was a business to them, after all.

Ivy came in and walked over to him, stroking his hair. Nigel closed his eyes. She knew just what he needed to feel better.

"I'm sorry, my love."

"I understand where he's coming from," Nigel said, putting his arms around Ivy's waist.

"Don't. You're a great inspector, provider and husband. He had no right to do that."

"It was his house. The delivery of the message may have been crude, but I get his point," Nigel continued and explained what went down with the Chief earlier.

Ivy shook her head. "Women are dead and they're more worried about the wealthy's reputations. They better be careful, lest the people take matters into their own hands."

Nigel exhaled. "Then we'll either need more coppers, or I'll be rich with all the overtime."

"Let's hope it doesn't get to that point."

A knock on the door interrupted them. Minnie stood there. "Mr. Lovelace is here."

Ivy stood and straightened her skirt. "The nerve of it!"

"He asked for Nigel," Minnie said, with a smile. "And he brought gifts."

CHAPTER 7

Nigel tilted his head as he went downstairs. Mr. Lovelace stood there, looking outside through the small window.

"Welcome, sir," Nigel said. "May I take your hat? Offer you a drink?"

Lovelace removed his hat and handed it to Nigel, who put it on the coat rack by the door. "Thank you, but I brought one," he said, holding up the brandy Nigel had given him.

Nigel gestured for Lovelace to join him in the sitting room. He walked over to the cabinet and got two glasses.

"I am here to apologize to you, lad. My manners during dinner were...undignified. I was out of line with you, a guest in my home," Lovelace said, and looked Nigel in the eye. "And a member of my family.

"What I heard from the Chief concerned me. There is a dark air over our land, Nigel, and that concerns me. But I didn't express myself correctly and insulted you. And for that, I am sorry."

Nigel swirled the brandy in his glass. "Like I told Ivy, I can understand where you're coming from, as I have my sister. It's not the same, but I sympathize. And apology accepted."

Lovelace nodded and raised the glass. "To family."

"To family."

Lovelace took a sip. "I say, this is not half bad."

"Thank you. It may not be as potent as you're used to, but those of us who enforce Her Majesty's justice need our wits about us. It allows me to relax after a trying day."

"I believe it," Mr. Lovelace said. He swilled his drink in the snifter a moment, then sat straight.

"I want to further express a desire to hire you."

"I beg your pardon?"

"My company is working on a new communications system, but we've hit a snag. I believe your brother Charles can help. It's a state-of-the-art feedback system. You won't even know it's there. I believe you saw Mortimer talking to your brother earlier."

So that was that unfortunate man Charles spoke to. Perhaps I was supposed to see that.

"These devices have another benefit as well. They can detect physiological changes in a person. If someone's heartbeat changes, an alarm will go off, which will send a telegram to my home."

"In theory anyway. That's where Charles comes in. If I could install the prototype here, I believe he can help us find what we're missing."

Lovelace poured himself another small swig of brandy. "What do you say?"

Nigel knew his father-in-law was putting his business on the line with this arrangement.

"Mr. Lovelace, I accept."

They shook hands. Nigel exhaled. *Now I have to tell Ivy.*

***

"No bloody way!" Ivy exclaimed, hands covering her mouth.

"It's wonderful. Charles is going to love it. He will have a new purpose. And the money will help with his care."

"Indeed! I just have one concern," Ivy mused aloud.

"What?"

"Who knows how sensitive he's going to make it? After all, my heart races when you touch me a certain way."

Nigel smiled.

"I wish there was a way we could see how he's setting this all up," Ivy continued.

"I wouldn't worry about that, dear," Nigel said, kissing her. "It just so happens you have a genius brother-in-law."

***

Nigel found Charles in his lab, working on an old lamppost lantern. Making his way towards the bench, he walked up on the side so that Charles could see him approach. At a young age, he learned the hard way the consequences of sneaking up on his brother. When they were kids, Charles stabbed him with a fork after he tried to scare him while Charles was eating porridge. Now that his brother had a menagerie of sharp objects in the lab, Nigel took no chances.

Charles looked up from his tinkering, reaching toward Nigel to grab a tool. He didn't acknowledge his sibling, just went about his work, even after Nigel cleared his throat.

"I understand you were quite busy at dinner. Did you have a good time?"

"Not every corner has light. Must brighten dark spaces."

Nigel took a deep breath. Normally, he didn't mind his brother's terseness, but when he needed to parse information from him, it could be a chore. To keep him from getting upset, Nigel considered it training for interrogating suspects and witnesses.

"That's very noble of you, Charles. Can you tell me what you spoke to Mr. Mortimer about?"

"New technology, new things. Lovelace rich off new things."

"Quite right, Charles. He furthers advances in technology. Is that why they roped you into helping?"

Charles put down the tool and looked at Nigel. "You can't upset the king and still be in his court."

He went back to his work and Nigel sat down. He referred to the history of Ivy's family. "That was her ancestor's doing, you know. Mr. Lovelace isn't responsible for that. He *is*, however, going to make some changes around here with your help. What are you helping with?"

"Eyes and ears, brother."

"Yes, I'm aware of what he's putting in here. He told me." Nigel shook his head. He wasn't getting anywhere. *Time to switch it up.* "You know, there's talk that Mr. Lovelace might receive a knighthood for his advancements in technology." Might get his titles back and a spot in the Royal Science Academy.

"That will give him the ability to sponsor promising individuals for apprenticeships. Don't suppose that came up?"

Charles turned to Nigel, the corners of his mouth twitching into a smile. "Latin is fun. Quid pro quo."

There it was. He promised something, which is how he got Charles to help. "Can't argue with that. I'd do the same. Now, what did he ask you to do?"

"Science. Science is the father of knowledge, but opinion breeds ignorance."

"Charles, please. What are you helping Ivy's dad with?" Nigel asked. After what seemed like hours but was likely closer to five minutes, Charles produced a piece of parchment from his pocket and held it out for Nigel, who took it. He opened it, revealing a wiring schematic. Although he didn't know the purpose of the device, he identified the dimensions for his house. He saw the wiring from the lab, through the kitchen and up to the bathroom and main bedroom. If Lovelace hadn't explained a bit about what he was doing, Nigel would be lost. Still, not a lot of this made much sense to him.

"Thank you, Charles," Nigel said, folding the paper and putting it next to his brother. "Though I do not know what it is or even how it works."

"Your new daddy does research," Charles said, not looking up. "You should too."

Nigel let that sink in a moment before leaving.

Ivy waited for him at the top of the stairs. "Miss me already?"

"You've got some company, darling," Ivy told him. Reginald stood in the doorway, hat removed. Nigel strode over and shook his hand. "I'm afraid you're too late, my good man. You missed the festivities."

"My apologies," Reginald said, but his frown suggested he wasn't in a joking mood. "Chief sent me over. You need to come with me."

"Just let me get my coat and hat."

"He said bring whatever tools you've got. We're going to need them."

CHAPTER 8

Reginald, known for being chatty, remained silent on the way over, only mentioning that they were going back to Camden Town and suspecting foul play. Pressing him for more didn't get him anywhere, as if something scared Reginald into silence.

Nigel felt a storm brewing inside him. He hoped that this could lead to more clues about who is harming these women. Perhaps this would implicate Ainsworth further – something even he felt was unlikely.

But if it *wasn't* the young aristocrat, then they had no real leads, and that upset Nigel's stomach to consider.

The carriage took them to Somers Town, an area of the city southeast of Camden Town. Nigel wasn't as familiar with this area of London. He knew that author Mary Shelley was born there, and that St. Parás, one of the oldest houses of worship in the whole of England, stood there.

They passed the church and turned down a rather nondescript street. It was full of row homes nudged together. Many of the lower working-class and servants of nobles lived on this street. In any of the homes, there could be three or four families living there.

The carriage stopped, and they disembarked. There was already a small crowd gathered, likely the residents. Many of Nigel's fellow inspectors and prescient bobbies were there, keeping them away from the alley.

Reginald moved through the gathered crowd, pushing residents out of the way who wouldn't budge. Nigel followed suit, not wanting to get left behind. He didn't have to move that fast, as Reginald stopped at the mouth of the alley, waiting for him.

"I want you to be prepared. I haven't seen anything like this and remember this is a young woman."

Nigel nodded. They each took a lantern from the police officer standing at the mouth of the alley. The other bobbies and inspectors inside parted as the two walked past. Nigel watched as two of the younger men gathered covered their mouths with a handkerchief. One of them appeared to be in tears.

Reginald stopped and turned to Nigel. "Here we are," he said, stepping back. And Nigel got a good look.

A young woman laid there on her back, arms and legs splayed. Her blonde, curly hair clung to her outfit. She had red clothing on, but a darker shade of red blood covered most of it. Nigel stepped forward, squatting down in front of the body. The stench of death assaulted his nostrils, but it didn't bother him as much as what he saw on the woman.

Nigel reached into his coat and pulled out a small cylinder. Twisting the end, it expanded to the length of his forearm. He used it to push away the fabric at her bosom.

"Nigel, that is most inappropriate," Reginald whispered.

"Look," Nigel said, moving the lantern over her chest. "Do you see the cuts?"

"Cuts? What cuts?"

"Right above her bosom."

Reginald leaned in, moving his lantern right next to Nigel's. His eyes followed Nigel's cylinder. Above her breast, there was a vertical slit of about two-to-three inches long. It was straight and precise, and Reginald said as much.

"The precision suggests these aren't random. She's not a mugging victim."

"So she knew her attacker."

"It's a reasonable assessment, but the others make me think there is something more."

"Others?" Reginald asked.

Nigel moved the cylinder over to the other side of the body, revealing a similar cut.

"My word, who would do that?"

"A collector of a sort," Nigel said, lifting the cylinder and moving it to the late woman's torso. There was a cut in the fabric. Nigel moved the cylinder around and found a third cut.

"Good heavens," Reginald said. He noticed a couple of his colleagues moving toward the body. "For all that is decent, men, step away."

Reginald watches the men as they step back. He turns back to Nigel. "The temerity."

"Are you saying that about this other cut?"

"A fourth! What kind of monster would do that?"

"These are deliberate, like some sort of ritual."

"I cannot imagine anyone doing that," Reginald said. "Other than a doctor."

"No respectful physician who loses a patient would do this. I don't believe this happened here. But the precision of the cuts, the location, I can't say without measuring, but they seem to be an equal distance apart. And don't worry, I don't plan on confirming that here."

"I should hope not," Reginald said. "But what is the significance of the cuts if they are equidistant?"

"I can't speculate. We won't know more until we get a closer look at the body."

"I'll get on it," Reginald said, and walked back toward the street. Nigel stood, the odor of the body finally hitting him. He covered his nose, and his thoughts turned to Ivy and Minnie.

Nigel decided against a carriage ride home. He needed time to process what he saw, so he walked. He worried his superiors would see something amiss in him for the way he investigated. Nigel needed that to avoid losing control altogether. One look at the victim's face, and he pictured his Ivy, her green eyes wide with surprise and torment, looking back at him. Or his dear sister lying in the mess, her body cut up to be found by a street urchin. He swallowed hard against the bile rising in his throat.

Even now, as the chilly wind enveloped him, that someone would harm another human, in London, on his watch, made his blood boil. They were the center of the world, the apex of modern civilization, and these atrocities were simply unacceptable here.

His thoughts reverted to the cuts on the late girl's body. The precision, the exact measurements stayed with Nigel. That convinced him that there was a reason for them. He'd have to wait, of course, but at the very least, he could start the report of his findings, thanks to Charles installing a telegraph machine in his lab.

Secrets. That word jumped around Nigel's brain, dancing in and out of thoughts. He'd have to delve deeper into this pattern, see if one existed here. Mr. Lovelace, who belonged to at least one club, would invariably know any secrets that organization had. It'd be a way into his good graces and prove his determination to do a good job. And if providing a little excitement for the old man helped, all the better. With renewed vigor, Nigel picked up the pace. He wanted to get his thoughts down so he could get rest.

The front door creaked as Nigel opened it, and he cursed himself for opening too fast. He sometimes forgot that late at night, or early in the morning or he treated coming home as the end of a regular day, not realizing the hour. He waited a moment before shutting the door, confident he had woken no one.

Nigel removed his coat and hat. He didn't feel any warmer as he put them away. He walked into the living room and saw the window was open. Pulling out the cylinder from the investigation, he twisted it, until it opened into the size of a cane.

Leaning against the wall, took a deep breath and returned to the living room, closing the window slowly. He approached the stairs and looked down at the first step, lifting his foot to step over it. *I have to get these creaks fixed.*

To keep his fear at bay and focus on staying as quiet as possible, he alternated his stance going up the stairs. With a tight grip on the cane, he paused at the top of the stairs. As he shifted to the left, he extended his hand towards the first door handle. Nigel let his hand linger on the handle before opening it. He lifted his cane above his head.

Charles lied there, shirtless, using scientific charts as covers. A light snore filled the air. Nigel shook his head. He looked at the window, which was closed. "Good night, dear brother," he whispered as he shut the door.

"What in blazes are you doing?" A voice whispered behind him. Nigel whipped around to see Minnie standing there, wiping sleep from her eyes.

"I came home and the downstairs window was open. I thought it prudent to make sure we were alone."

"By coming in our rooms?"

"You'd be thankful if I'd come across a perpetrator and subdued him. And pull your gown up."

Minnie looked down and her bosom almost spilled out of her gown. She made a noise as she pulled it up. "Please, no more excitement this evening."

She returned to her room, shutting the door with a loud thud. "You're welcome, sister," Nigel said as went to bed.

***

Nigel slept little that night. He could close his eyes, but soon after, he'd see the dead woman and her cuts. At first, he chalked it up to – what did Charles call it? – his subconscious – working on the puzzle of the deceased's incisions. But the woman's face would turn into Ivy's or Minnie's visage, and he'd sit up, heart pounding, nightshirt soaked with perspiration.

He got some shut eye just as the sun rose in his window, but a pounding on his door woke him up what seemed like minutes later.

He shot up in bed. Once he got his bearings, he looked for his wife, but remembered Ivy was visiting her mother today.

Nigel let his legs drag onto the floor and sauntered to the door. He opened it to find Minnie there, properly dressed this time. Though now her brow furrowed and her hands were stuck to her hips.

"What is it?"

"A visitor."

"Who?"

"One of your fellow coppers."

I can't imagine there is a break in the case already. I barely got any sleep.

"And would you put a robe on?" Minnie said, imitating his tone the night before. She winked and smiled.

"Right," Nigel said, hustling to his room to grab his overcoat. He put it on as he descended the stairs.

"Good morning sir," the young officer said. He had freckles and red hair that was speckled with gray. Nigel received a warm nod from the rookie, whose eyes glowed with kindness.

"Hello, Edward," Nigel said, shaking his colleague's hand. "Fancy seeing you on this side of town."

"My sister lives nearby, sir," Edward said. "She just had her first baby, a boy."

"Congratulations," Nigel said, clapping Edward's shoulder. "Healthy?"

"As a horse, sir."

"Excellent," Nigel said. "I gather you're not here for a social call."

"You're correct, sir," Edward said, pulling a piece of paper from his right jacket pocket, handing it Nigel.

He recognized Chief Willoughby's writing at once, with the exaggerated hoops on his G's and H's.

Inspector, please leave for the precinct as soon you have received this letter. I need you on a case post haste.

Nigel tried to hide his smile as he folded the note. "Thank you, Edward. I will be there in the blink of an eye."

Edward nodded and walked out.

He turned and bound for the stairs, but Minnie stepped in front of him.

"I heard," she said. "Good news?"

"It sure is," Nigel told her. "Think the chief wants me to lead the investigation."

"Brilliant. Before you go, can you tell Charles to put a shirt on?"

Nigel rolled his eyes and hustled outside. Sure enough, Charles stood there, *sans* shirt, but he had pants on, to Nigel's relief. Charles also wore a top hat. He stood by a carriage, hands on his hips, looking at the crates.

"What are you doing?"

"New science is here."

"New science?"

"From our other daddy."

"Ah," Nigel said. Lovelace's new communications system. Nigel had half a thought to find it and accidentally drop it.

There were a few onlookers about, which didn't bother Nigel, at first. His neighbors mostly stayed out his affairs, and he reciprocated. But as Nigel looked longer, he realized they were looking at Charles.

"Can you work on the new system without your lab coat?"

Charles's eyes grew wide. "Must be ready," he said, running into the house.

"Thank you," Nigel said, taking a crate from the coachmen.

He put it on the table in the lab. Charles was already putting items on the table, figuring out their purpose. Nigel smiled. He loved seeing Charles in his element. One day, he'd be a fly on the wall to appreciate his brother's talents.

Not today, though. The Chief had important work for him.

***

"Nigel," Willoughby said, "This is Mrs. Pemberton."

An old woman stood across the desk from Nigel at the precinct. Hunched over, clothes loose around her thin frame, Nigel guessed she must have been around seventy. Her eyes appeared to be stuck in a perpetual squint.

"Good morning, Mrs. Pemberton," Nigel said, still not sure what was going on.

"Mrs. Pemberton wishes to report a crime," Willoughby said, looking at Nigel. "Please take her statement."

Willoughby turned away to other business. Nigel blinked and pursed his lips. Taking a deep breath, he turned to Mrs. Pemberton and forced a smile.

"Come with me, Mrs. Pemberton," Nigel said, leading her into the first open office, holding a chair out for her. He sat across from her and produced a pen and notepad from his pocket.

"Now, can you tell me what happened?"

"A bird demon."

Nigel's pen fell from his hand. "I, I beg your pardon?"

"A bird demon," Mrs. Pemberton repeated.

"A bird demon," Nigel said. "Can you describe it?"

"Would you be so kind to stand for me?"

Nigel exhaled loudly. "This is getting peculiar," he mumbled to himself, standing.

Mrs. Pemberton's eyes opened slightly. "It came up to your chin. It wore a dress, with a big skirt and its face was a beak."

Nigel wrote this down. "Did you see its eyes? Was it holding anything in its...talons?"

Mrs. Pemberton shook her head. "It was dark and the lamps were low on fuel. They were all black. Oh, and they didn't have talons. At least, I don't think so. They had gloves."

"I see," Nigel said, taking notes. "So all black, no color, gloves. And what were they doing?"

"Walking."

Nigel put the pad down. "Just walking?"

"Yes, but it scared Mr. Bellevue next door, and poor Katherine Kane screamed with fright."

"Was Ms. Kane attacked?"

"Oh no, her father came out and chased the beast away."

"So it did nothing?"

"It's frightening, Officer Barrington," Mrs. Pemberton scolded. "And it should be stopped."

"Inspector," Nigel said under his breath. "Mrs. Pemberton, there are a lot of frightening things in the world. But until these things hurt someone, bird demons or otherwise, I'm afraid there isn't much we can do."

Mrs. Pemberton tapped her cane on the floor. "I will hold you to that, young man."

She leaned forward to stand, and Nigel got up to help her. He led her, without further word, to the front door.

"Thank you so much for coming in, Mrs. Pemberton," Nigel said, helping her down the steps. "Please do let us know if these bird demons show up again and cause any trouble."

"Of course, officer," Mrs. Pemberton said as she walked away, then stopped and turned around. "Oh, officer!"

Nigel huffed. "Yes?" he asked, turning to her.

"When they moved by a lamp, their dressed billowed in the wind and I glimpsed a pink petticoat."

"Pink petticoat," Nigel said. "Got it."

He turned and walked up the stairs, to see Reginald blocking his path wearing a sullen face.

"Hello Reginald."

"We've got another one."

"Another young woman?"

"No. A young noble."

CHAPTER 9

The carriage hit a bump, and Nigel steadied himself. He was on the edge of the seat, moving about every few seconds. Reginald watched the whole affair, and if it bothered him, he didn't show it.

"You said it's not far?" Nigel asked, and Reginald shook his head. "It's not Lord Ainsworth?" Another head shake.

Nigel sat back, allowing himself a moment to relax. He glanced at Reginald, surprised at how melancholy his colleague and friend looked. He wanted to ask him about it but felt it prudent to wait.

"I'm surprised Willoughby-"

"He didn't. After your...confrontation with Ainsworth, he didn't want you anywhere near this case."

"And yet-"

"They've given me full authority, using whatever tools I can. You're the best of us inspectors."

Nigel tried to talk, but nothing came out. A quiet grunt was all he could manage. His face felt flush a moment, something he'd seen on Ivy when he proposed. *You're a good man, Reginald.*

"Then how, exactly, am I to keep my involvement a secret?"

"I'll report directly to Willoughby, and the findings will be a group effort, albeit one I spearheaded. However, I ask that you don't wear your stovepipe hat."

"Understood, but it *is* nighttime in Fall. In London."

Reginald's lips curved upward for a moment. He reached into his pocket and produced a flat cap, in black.

Nigel took his stovepipe hat off and put on the flat cap. To his surprise, it fit snug enough, but not too tight, and he said as much. "Did the missus pick this out for you?"

"You have the biggest head of anyone I've ever seen. I asked for the largest one they had."

"I cannot decide if I'm proud or offended."

"You're an inspector. You'll figure it out."

Nigel took the cap and slapped Reginald's arm. Reginald chuckled for a moment, then his face became serious. "We're here."

Reginald got out and turned back to the carriage. "Stay close to me. Oh, and put this on, too. You're sensitive to the smell."

Nigel took the handkerchief. It was rather large, like the hat, but he smiled, as it was big enough to tie around his face. Putting on his gloves, he exited the carriage. Staying to Reginald's right, he kept his head down.

He recognized the spire atop Crosby Hall at the far end of the street. They were in Chelsea. Reginald greeted his colleagues with a nod. *I can't believe they don't recognize me. I'll have to keep this in mind.*

Reginald led him to a home that had two stories of the brick matching Crosby Hall. Its bottom windows were as tall as Nigel and nearly as wide.

Panicked people stood outside, consoling each other. Their clothing, stained with dirt and sweat, showed they were the household staff. A couple of well-dressed folks, Nigel guessed middle-aged, also gathered, watching the bobbies, and chatting. Clearly nobles, but Nigel didn't know if they were family of the victim or calling on the deceased.

Nigel leaned toward Reginald's ear. "We might want to detain those finely dressed gentlemen."

Reginald nodded and called over a Constable. Nigel turned around, taking in the scene as Reginald spoke to the constable. The walk is pristine, as is the lawn and fountain, decorated with a marble statue of a mermaid spewing water from her mouth.

"Follow me," Reginald said.

Even with a larger doorway, Nigel ducked as he entered, a force of habit. Some of his colleagues watched as he did so. Recalling that he had Reginald's flat cap on, he wanted to straighten up, look proper, but moved closer to the doorway, pretending to examine them for clues.

The inside was as large as Nigel expected, the ceiling about two and half times his height. Marble was everywhere: in the foyer, on the walls, even in the dressing rooms. Large paintings, hung on the walls. He noticed modern conveniences in the living area, including one of the first Babbage radios, directly from the factory.

None of Nigel's colleagues were in this area, so he kept his gawking to a minimum and followed Reginald back to the kitchen. Reginald stepped to his right as he walked in, eyeing the table in the middle. A man's body lay there, arms splayed above his head facing the far wall. There was a knife protruding from his back. The only thing he wore was a patterned smoking jacket, predominately red, the same color as the blood pooling on the table.

Nigel moved forward, stepping around the two constables cataloguing the room, their faces covered with handkerchiefs. The smell of death was enveloping, muting the aroma of anything else that might have been wafting through the kitchen. A few items were strewn about the floor. Nigel recognized salt and a canister of sugar. On the opposite side of the table, the oven was off, but bread and a meat – Nigel guessed mutton – sat undisturbed.

Reginald walked beside Nigel. "These are the remains of Baron Chesterfield, aged twenty-seven years," he said, checking his notes. Eyeing the knife, he continued, "I believe you can discern the cause of death."

Nigel nodded and then gestured toward the corpse.

"Please," Reginald said. He stepped around the body, almost tripping on a fireplace poker that lay between the body and the stove. Reginald watched with interest.

An inspector came in, carrying a hand-held version of Flamming's Revolving camera. Nigel recalled Charles had seen one in a photobook of the American West once, and had tried to build his own, but didn't have the parts. Like the regular version, it featured a mahogany body, black fabric balance, brass trim, and lens. It just fit in the inspector's palm.

Nigel stepped back toward Reginald, letting the photographer work. "Amazing piece of equipment."

"One of the first. Willoughby let me have it, to my surprise."

"Who was the victim?" Nigel asked.

"Third generation aristocrat, not much for social activities. Rumor is he spent time in the opium dens, amongst less than respectable company."

"His status ensures that this rumor remains just that," Nigel commented, watching his colleague take a variety of photographs.

"Having powerful friends doesn't hurt either," Reginald said. "Like Lord Rushforth."

Nigel raised an eyebrow. "I'm surprised he's not here yet."

"I thought we weren't in the business of informing friends and acquaintances, but I'm sure that the Chief will have him here before long. Which is why I want this solved as quickly as possible."

The photographer finished and nodded to Reginald. "On my way now, sir. Top priority."

"That's a good lad." He turned to Nigel. "There aren't any prints. Someone was careful, and given the victim, I can understand why. Therefore, it's likely to be pre-meditated."

"Servants?" Nigel asked.

"The lord gave them the night off, save for his majordomo, who was in his quarters in the opposite wing.

"Or, considering the company the Baron kept, the killer had a tendency to wear gloves."

Nigel stepped forward and examined the knife. Other than the blood droplets that hit it, it was as clean and shiny as if it was just washed.

"Do you have a light?" Nigel asked, and Reginald turned around, snapping his fingers. A young bobbie came in, carrying a large, clumsy Bullseye Lantern. Reginald brought it over.

"For Heaven's sake," Reginald cried, "My apologies, this old thing has a candle."

"That's quite all right. I just want a closer look. Do you mind putting out the rest of the lights?"

Reginald snapped his fingers. "You heard the man."

The gathered cops did as ordered and Nigel took off the lid, which was creased like a handkerchief in someone's hand. He lit the candle inside, replacing the lid. The bulb, which was large, and resembled the stop lights Charles had read about, turned orange. It illuminated a cone-shaped distance of around six feet, and he moved closer to the body. The lantern was hot, Nigel already feeling the heat in his hands, despite his gloves.

Nigel turned his focus to the body and what the fiery light would show him. The light was brighter than he expected, and he closed his eyes and reopened them to better adjust to his surroundings.

He couldn't see anything new upon re-inspection. The knife was still clean, no prints. Somehow it got into the Baron's back, and nothing here gave any clues how.

Wait. What's that?

At the small of the Baron's back, a shadow showed in the light. It wasn't much, but it was something. Nigel looked to the closest bobbie, a man of about forty, with a Fu Manchu-style moustache and pointed to the shadowed mass.

"You there, get that small lump for me, please?" The man walked over, leaned forward near the Baron's buttocks, then shuffled to the left when he recognized how close he was to a corpse's bare posterior. He reached for the lump.

"No," Nigel said, as the Bobbie recoiled. "Not with your hands! It might have evidence on it!"

Bringing it over to Nigel, The bobbie produced a handkerchief from his pocket and wrapped it up.

Enclosed within the handkerchief were two pieces of fabric, with one piece being a brown shade of leather. It seemed to Nigel that the second item he discovered was a piece of clothing. Its look was somewhat worn yet not entirely new. He gave them to Reginald. "Get this to the lab post haste!"

A commotion filled the air, and Reginald turned towards it. Men shouted, and a couple of bobbies strode toward the commotion. Reginald moved forward as well.

Nigel turned the lantern off. "Turn the lights on." No one moved. We should assess the need for self-defense."

The bobbies opened them up, just in time for Lord Ainsworth to run in. "Where's the Baron?"

He stopped in his tracks as he saw the body. He turned while Nigel removed his hat and pulled his collar down.

CHAPTER 10

"Lord Ainsworth," Reginald said, stepping between Nigel and the noble. "It's best if you're not here."

"He's my friend. What happened?"

"Now's not the time, my lord."

"I *demand* to know what happened!"

Nigel popped around Reginald. "I'm afraid we can only inform immediate family at this time."

Ainsworth paced, trying to see the body, but Reginald did his best to block him. The young aristocrat tried to get around him, only to run into Nigel. Reginald waved a hand and two Bobbies came over. Ainsworth saw the two men, sighed and walked out with them.

Adjusting his face covering, Nigel tailed the officers outside, waiting at the entrance until the bobbies returned to the house before approaching Ainsworth.

"Might I have a moment of your time?" Nigel asked, taking the handkerchief off his face.

"Look, I already-"

Ainsworth froze when he turned and saw Nigel standing there. "I swear to you I had nothing to do with this."

"Fret not, my Lord, I am not here to harangue you. Though it *is* curious why you're here in less than half a day from the time of death."

"He died within the past few hours?"

"A very excellent observation, Lord Ainsworth. I expected nothing less from a man of your background. But those words didn't come from my mouth. How *did* you find out about this?"

Ainsworth turned to the two nobles that had entered the room.

"Those gentlemen informed you?"

"Yes, we all meet at a social club on Wednesdays for cards and brandy."

"I see. I've seen them about but can't recall their names."

"Duke Hammersmith and Lord Fleming."

"Thank you for your cooperative manner, Lord Ainsworth. Might I suggest, given recent events, you not dally about the grounds much longer."

"Agreed, Inspector. Good day."

Nigel watched Ainsworth go and motioned to an inspector standing near the entrance. The young man, whom Nigel recognized as Matthew, came over. He tried to look stern and nonchalant, but he was on edge, and needed to take a deep breath. Nigel made sure the scarf still covered his face, ensuring Matthew didn't recognize him.

"The boss wants to talk to them," Nigel said, looking at Hammersmith and Entwistle. "Tell me we have a place for them."

Matthew let out that breath as he looked around. "I don't know, sir. All the areas I would think we can use are occupied."

"We're certainly taking advantage of the space, aren't we," Nigel said, and Matthew smiled. "Why not ask the boss? I'll start working those two."

Matthew nodded and took a step, then stopped. He furrowed his brow. "Forgive me, sir, but you look rather familiar. Do I know you?"

Nigel felt himself tense up, He took a breath, concealed beneath his collar, so his junior colleague couldn't see.

"The Chief calls me to help once in a while. I should get over there in case they think they can leave."

"Right," Matthew said, and headed for the house.

Nigel eyed the nobles, who were talking to one another and one of the late noble's servants. Careful not to make eye contact, Nigel walked around the fountain in the middle of the courtyard, making his way next to them.

Duke Hammersmith, at least outwardly, personified what a commoner expected a noble to be: tailored suit, well-groomed, an air of grace and class, even standing still. Nigel caught a faint whiff of an evergreen tree.

The servant bowed and excused himself. Nigel put his collar down, looking at the house. He wanted to seem casual, not that he was stalking them for information.

"A terrible tragedy, this is," Nigel said.

"Indeed," Hammersmith said.

"Are you family?"

"Not in the blood sense," Fleming replied, turning his head to look at Nigel. "What about you?"

Nigel shook his head. "Just a concerned citizen. If people take out the top of society, what hope does the common man have?"

The nobles approved with a nod and a quick smile. Nigel hid a grin. *Getting a witness to talk does not differ from courting a woman, Willoughby once said. It's just your subject isn't as appealing.*

Nigel saw Matthew in the doorway. The lad had enough sense to see who Nigel was talking to and nodded. Nigel adjusted his head, implying that Matthew should come by. Matthew caught on and strode over.

"Gentlemen, if you wish to pay your respects to the deceased, the head inspector said you may have a few moments."

"Mighty kind of him," Fleming said.

"Indeed, lad. Thank you," Hammersmith said.

"Follow me," Matthew said and led them inside.

Nigel waited until they were halfway to the entrance before walking in. He took high strides, to the point of looking ridiculous, almost as if he was stepping over something every few centimeters. Only one or two people looked at him, but did their best to steer clear. *Good, maybe my eccentricity will continue to deter people from conversing with me.*

He kept Matthew in his sights, as he led the two nobles into a room. Nigel nodded as he entered and closed the door.

Three chairs stifled the small office, akin to a lender's office at the Royal Bank. The nobles sat on the "customer" side of the desk. Nigel walked around and took his place opposite.

He removed his cap and lowered his collar. "Gentlemen, I am Nigel Barrington, Inspector in Her Majesty's Police Force. Thank you for making time for me today."

"Where is our friend?" Hammersmith said.

"I say, this is most irregular," Fleming said. "They promised us time to pay our respects."

"You will, I assure you," Nigel said. "We didn't say *what time* you'd be able to do that."

"I won't abide this," Hammersmith said, standing. "You will release me this instant."

"I can do that," Nigel said, "And I can also inform the head Inspector on the case that you weren't willing to answer a few simple questions about your relationship to the deceased. This will cause my superior to wonder if you had something to do with this, as my notes will suggest."

Fleming huffed, and Hammersmith let out an elongated, annoyed sigh as he returned to his seat. "Your superior will hear about this," Hammersmith said.

"He'll be glad to know I followed proper procedures. Time of year for raises, and all."

"Now, you two frequented the same club as the deceased, is that correct?" The men nodded. "And what was the name of the club?"

"The London Buck," Hammersmith said. "We shared stories, brandy, games."

Nigel held his cap, twirling it in his hands. "Such as?"

"Cards, and the usual fare," Fleming said. "Is that all?"

"Did you often frequent each other's homes?"

"Occasionally, but we haven't been there in months."

Nigel opened his mouth to continue, but a knock on the door interrupted him.

Reginald stood there. "Forgive me gentleman." He looked at Nigel. "May I speak to you?"

Nigel excused himself and stepped outside. Reginald stood there, wearing a look of weariness. "The interrogation's over."

"But-"

Reginald held up a finger and pointed to the entrance. Lord Rushforth stood there, chatting with the same servant Hammersmith and Fleming mingled with.

"Of all the...Reginald, I'm almost done."

"I'm sorry, Nigel. Willoughby's one rule was that I don't upset Rushforth."

"Fine, You can give them the news. I have to go," Nigel said as left, cap on his head. He was uncomfortably close to the nobles as they exited the manor.

Rushforth's too close to all of this for my liking. I'm going to figure out what he's up to, Heaven help me.

***

Reginald arranged for Nigel to take his carriage home, which was his way of apologizing for what happened.

"I'll update you post haste," Reginald said, before the carriage left.

Nigel used the trip home to open his notebook and jot down his findings. The lack of any markings on the body or the murder weapon were of keen interest. *The victim knew his killer, or at least invited them into the house.*

But how did they leave nary a print, or a sign of their time inside? That thought stuck with Nigel. Even the most meticulously clean person leaves a trace or dirt or scuff occasionally. Why wasn't that the case? The servants surely weren't cleaning when the victim was entertaining. That would be improper.

Improper.

Nigel leaned back in the carriage chair. Of course! The victim was in his evening wear, his robe, without pants. He wasn't only entertaining, he wanted to be entertained himself. The question is, was it a man or woman he shared company with?

The carriage stopped just as he scribbled the last note and pocketed the book. The coachmen opened the door and Nigel thanked him, giving him halfpence before running into his home.

***

He didn't expect raucous laughter when he got home, but it filled his ears, startling him enough to drop the hat when he tried to hang it. "What in the world?"

Nigel headed toward the sound, finding its source in the kitchen. Minnie sat there with the bobbie from the investigation, the one with the Fu Manchu mustache. She tapped his forearm and throws her head back laughing, before sipping tea. Nigel clears his throat, and the Bobbie's smile disappears. He almost falls out of his chair trying to stand up.

"Hello, Nigel," Minnie said, coughing out the tea she just sipped as Nigel entered. "Archibald here was just telling me funny stories about the job."

"That so?" Nigel said, turning his attention to Archibald, who stood straight as a board.

Nigel clasped his hand behind his back, bobbing up and down on his feet before steadying himself. He wanted to give his junior colleague the benefit of the doubt and assume that he was here with a message from Reginald. And his sister was young, available, and she was attractive.

But walking in to see the Archibald getting close and comfortable gave the opposite impression. And while Nigel had every right to protest and show the young man out, his current status at the department made him think twice.

"Your sister invited me in, Inspector."

"That's mighty kind of her. She is an exceptional hostess."

"Indeed, sir," Archibald said, keeping his expression blank. "Excellent tea."

"Quite so. Speaking of which, Minnie, would you mind making me some? I'd like the leaves from Granderson's. I believe that's downstairs."

She stood and said to Archibald, "Please excuse me."

She took her leave.

"Sir, I wasn't doing anything untoward, I assure you."

"I've believe you, Archibald. Though I am surprised to see you here I heard there was a murder."

"That's the reason for my visit, sir. Inspector Coates told me to come to you. I was to take something to the lab, but they wouldn't look at it."

"Why not?"

"The piece comes from a mask of some kind, from a masquerade ball. It's leather. He recognized it from one his sister's family threw last year."

"Thank you very much, Archibald."

"Happy to help Inspector. Have a great evening. And thank your sister for the company and the tea."

Nigel stared daggers at Archibald, who nodded and took his leave.

Sitting in Archibald's vacated chair, Nigel stared at the small piece of leather. He now had another avenue to explore in the case.

A loud clanging and scraping of metal on wood filled his ears and his thoughts evaporated. He covered his ears, but the noise penetrated the fleshly shield, and Nigel moved toward it. The closer he got to the bottom of the stairs, the more obvious it became. Charles was up to something. *It sounded heavy and expensive.*

Nigel waited at the base of the stairs, moving only when the secret door opened toward him. He waited for his brother with arms crossed and a scowl. Nigel replaced his attempts to showcase his disappointment with curiosity as Charles pulled a cylinder upstairs. The scraping, in open air, penetrated Nigel's ears even more, so he moved over and helped him. It contained brass and copper components. Nigel imagined that carrying Minnie and his wife wouldn't be as taxing. He did not know what was inside; that was Charles's purview. Charles led them to the kitchen, and they set it on the table. *It's almost my birthday. Maybe I'll even get a straight answer for once.*

They set it down, and Charles, to Nigel's delight, was careful not to let it slam down. He wagered Charles cared more about the device than the table, but a win is a win.

"Obliged," Charles said, wiping his face with his lab coat, now stained with sweat and grime.

"What do we have here?" Nigel asked.

"Something new," Charles whispered, smiling. Nigel smiled too. He enjoyed seeing his brother smile. It didn't happen often, given his condition.

"And heavy. I trust you don't plan on keeping it where we eat."

"Silly. Goes into office. For office things."

That's crazy, Charles, which says something. "Not without you telling me what it does."

"Monitor."

"I don't understand how you can see anything with this."

"Not view. Catalogue, record."

"Oh, I see. And what can it record?"

"Whatever we want. New Daddy wants it to record telegraphs."

"So Mr. Lovelace sent this?"

Charles shook his head. "His box is simple, small. Needed something bigger."

"To monitor the telegraphs."

Again, Charles shakes his head. "Everything."

Nigel raises an eyebrow. "What do you mean, everything?"

Charles taps the cylinder. "We can monitor anything we program. Our New Daddy wants telegraphs. But you protect, serve. You need to monitor notes, cases, people."

"That's impressive, Charles. Thank you."

"Like Minnie."

"What about her?"

"You can monitor why she leaves after I go night-night."

— · —

CHAPTER 11

Nigel knocked once before entering Minnie's room. She sat at her table, using the brass knobs to tighten her corset. Her shoulders were bare, and she looked at Nigel wide-eyed and emitted a quick scream.

"What in bloody hell are you doing? Get out!"

"One, I knocked. Two, it's not anything I haven't seen. Three, it's your shoulders. Get dressed. We need to talk."

Minnie huffed, but tossed a shawl over her shoulders, exaggerating her movements while pouting. Nigel recalled her doing this when she was younger to curry favor from their late father, and to their mother's chagrin, it often worked. Nigel was no fool and said as much.

"I don't appreciate you barging in here," Minnie said.

"*I* don't appreciate learning of your nightly activities."

Minnie stopped. "What are you talking about?"

Nigel motioned for her to follow him. Downstairs, Charles was wiping down the cylinder. Minnie winced at the sight of it.

"That's ghastly. What is it?"

"It's a device to record things. For example," he said, turning to Charles. "Charles, tell Minnie what this thing can do for her."

"Naughty," Charles said, not looking up. "Leave after wolf howls at midnight."

"What?"

"You're sneaking out, Minnie."

"Unconscionable! Why I-"

Nigel crossed his arms and stared at her.

"Okay fine. I do."

"Lord in Heaven, Minnie. Do you know-"

"Sod off, Nigel. You're not dad."

"I'm responsible for you and keeping our family name respectable. With all the murders going on, you could get hurt, or worse."

"Good heavens. You want to know what I'm doing? Come on."

***

They stood outside a dress shop about a mile away. The exterior painted red, the signs in red as well. Minnie didn't say a word as she walked in. Nigel followed her.

The store was clean, as if it just opened its doors to the public. The dresses were pristine, in a variety of colors and shapes. Minnie weaved in and out of the dresses on her way to the counter. Nigel tried to keep up, but he had trouble navigating the hoop skirts and rows of frilly lace. No doubt expensive; the entire precinct would have a hard time paying for the store's inventory.

Nigel made it through, all dresses still intact. He saw Minnie chatting with a lovely, round woman behind the counter. The purple dress hugged her figure so well, as if made just for her. It moved when she moved, like an extension of her skin, not a garment. She laughed with Minnie as she hemmed a dress.

"Winifred, you remember me talking about my brother?" Minnie looked at him.

"He doesn't look ill."

Nigel huffed.

"No, this is the copper."

"Oh, the mighty upholder of Her Majesty's Law," Winifred said. She looked at Minnie. "He's big, all right. I'm not sure I have anything in his size off the rack."

Minnie looked at Nigel and laughed. "Oh no, he couldn't pull that off."

"Excuse me!"

"Would you be so kind as to show my brother what you're making for me? You know, the dress you're designing after hours for me, that requires my input?"

"Of course. Just let me finish this." She tied a stitch at the end of a dress hem and set it down. "If you'd be so kind, please follow me."

Minnie held the door for Nigel, a smirk of victory on her face. Nigel ignored it as he followed Winifred through a door marked "private". She lumbered down a corridor past the office. Behind him, Minnie hummed a tune. Nigel turned and scowled. She smiled back and kept humming.

Winifred waited for them at the end of the hallway, hand on a door. She pushed it, gesturing for Nigel to enter. Inside, wall-to-wall racks of dresses filled the room, a kaleidoscope of color.

I'm not sure I've ever seen some of these colors before. Minnie bumped into him as she walked by. She smiled, putting an extra spring in her step. Clearly, she was enjoying his lack of comfort.

Nigel took careful note of where Minnie walked and followed her path. Her smaller frame enabled her to weave in and out of the racks, but Nigel, being wider, had to turn parallel to the racks to sidestep some of them.

The room was the proprietor's office, comprising a small desk, a floor length Difference Engine behind the desk, and reams of fabric set up on the walls.

Looks like a mechanical abacus, Nigel thought as he looked at the Difference Engine.

Winifred gestured for them to sit and Nigel stepped behind Minnie's chair, pulling it out.

"There you are, sister."

"Thank you, brother," sarcasm in her voice. "Not sure what I'd do without you."

"A great question."

Nigel took a seat next to her as Winifred opened a door behind her desk. It was a walk-in closet, one that was generous in its size. *Something this size would surely impress even Rushforth.*

Winifred came out with a dress on a hanger, carrying it like a newborn baby. The dress was pink. Nigel didn't know why, but he recalled seeing one similar before, but not as bright. *Maybe it's like one Minnie has. Though it appears to bring back memories of Charles getting sick from eating shellfish on holiday as kids.*

Nigel noted this dress had long sleeves, and buttons down the middle of it. A brown material was visible inside the skirt, which he thought was leather and wondered that aloud.

"It's a petticoat, Officer," Winifred said, pulling it up to the counter.

"Inspector, and thank you."

"My apologies, Inspector."

"No need, ma'am," Nigel said, leaning on the desk to take a closer look. There was a floral design on the dress, including the jacket. It was a swirling pattern.

"I'm not familiar with this type of flower, Winifred. Is it native to Britain?"

Minnie snorted, which caused Winifred to smile, but she wiped the grin away once Nigel focused on her. "That's not quite a flower, Inspector. It's paisley, a Persian design."

"It's unique. This is excellent work."

"Thank you."

"*Now* do you believe me, brother?"

"I do, but one thing bugs me."

Minnie put her hands on her hips and gestured for him to continue.

"Why are you sneaking out so late?"

"I'm afraid that's my fault, Inspector," Winifred said. "I'm just a seamstress here, but I have grand designs on having my own dress line. It's very hard for anyone to take me seriously, given where I am. And I can only focus on my own designs at night.

"I didn't want to approach you about it until they were ready. Your sister has no doubts you'd be willing to pay when they're done."

"Did she now?" Nigel mused. Times were changing and progress was coming about, but even Minnie seemed to skirt the normal levels of propriety at times.

"Minnie is giving me a chance," Winifred said, not making eye contact with Nigel. "I hope you will, too."

"I must apologize, Minnie. The dress looks lovely, Winifred. What is it for?"

"Right now, I'll use this for social engagements."

"A wise decision," Winifred said, turning her attention to Nigel. "I'd hate to scrap this design, given what it will cost once it's all done."

Nigel perked up. "How much *does* it cost?"

Winifred handed him a tag that was on the dress. Nigel felt the color drain from his face and out of the corner of his eye, he saw Minnie's toothy grin.

***

Nigel held the door open for Minnie into their home. She smiled the entire way back from Winifred's shop.

Minnie eyed him as she walked inside. "What a lovely day," she said.

"You're being incorrigible," Nigel told her.

"This is the way of things. You just got lucky, nabbing Ivy before her debut."

"I had the privilege of having a reputable job when we met."

"That's not all you had," Ivy said, coming out from the kitchen, sipping tea. "What's the ruckus?"

Minnie relayed the information on the dress and Nigel's surprise at the cost. "Minnie doesn't need help, dear," Ivy said. "But it doesn't hurt to put your best foot forward. You should have seen what mother planned for me."

"You would have looked exquisite," Nigel said.

"I can't wait to find someone to speak like that to me," Minnie daydreamed aloud.

"In due time," Nigel said. "I can't think about that right now." He relayed the Bird Demons and the aristocratic murder.

"The weirdest thing," he continued, "Is that her eyes, almost per-manently closed, could see pink under a black dress in the dark night. It'd have to be a strong wind to move the skirt enough for her to see pink on the demon's petticoat."

Nigel looked up at Ivy, who shot a quick glance to Minnie. He sat up straight, and opened his mouth to call them on it, but he heard a faint buzzing in the air. He moved toward the hallway, and the noise changed. *Tap, tap, tink, tink.*

The telegraph device spat out a message, then shut down. Nigel picked it up as Ivy entered. "Did it work?"

"Yes," Nigel said, reading. "It appears I'm to come to the station straight away."

"Splendid," Ivy said, reading the printout. "Could this put you back on the noble's case?"

"If they want to end these murders, they'd better."

"Do hurry home," Ivy said. "This confidence of yours is making my corset a tad tight. I think it needs to come off."

"Far be it from me to argue with a reasonable request. See you as soon as I can."

***

The station wasn't bristling with activity like Nigel expected. A few bobbies were about, doing their work. Reginald wasn't there, and Nigel asked the officer of his whereabouts, who thought he was in with Willoughby.

This is a good sign. Nigel straightened, his walk morphing from calculated steps made in fear to ones of cautious optimism. He fixed his collar and tugged on his coat. No sense in leaving anything to chance; if he had to debate or coerce, Nigel would look his best.

He knocked on Willoughby's door and a baritone voice invited him in. His boss sat at his desk, leaning forward, hands merged as if praying. Reginald was sitting opposite him, his notebook and folders on his lap, expression blank. Nigel could gauge what Reginald felt, be it a raised eyebrow or flaring nostrils. Now, he couldn't tell anything.

"Inspector Barrington."

"You wanted to see me, sir?"

"My wife likes to inform me that as the days pass, my memory is becoming as foggy as a fall evening in London. So maybe I am guilty of that here, but I recall telling you to stick to police work required of your position of inspector."

Nigel let that hang for a moment.

"Correct me if I am wrong, but this should allow you to conduct the duties required by your position, do they not?"

"I believe so, sir."

"While I consider you stubborn, I don't take you for a simpleton. Are you a simpleton, Barrington?"

"Depends on who you ask, sir," Nigel said. Willoughby stared at him. "No sir."

"Then why do I get a visit from concerned parties, saying that you trespassed on their property, accusing them of impropriety? A case which you were told to hand off, as the priority was the murder of local English lords?"

"I was never told to hand it off, sir. The priority-"

"I'm aware of my own words, Inspector. You don't need to regurgitate them," Willoughby said, taking a deep breath, so his face would lose its red tinge.

"Her Majesty charters us. Everything we do reflects on her. You disobeyed me, and you accused upstanding citizens of criminal activity."

"I did no such-"

Willoughby raised a hand. "By proxy, you are saying the Queen accuses these people. Not only that, you did this despite being expressly forbidden from doing so. I will keep your badge and revoking your privileges forthwith. You are hereby suspended without pay for one week, and you will return demoted to a bobbie. And if I hear of *any* activity relating to any cases you worked on, I will bring the fullest extent of the law down upon you."

Willoughby turned to Reginald. "This includes consulting with any upstanding, model inspectors in this precinct. Am I understood?"

"Sir."

Nigel turned and walked out.

***

Nigel stopped outside and exhaled as he left the station, taking one last look at the building. The place that had been his home for years – until Ivy came into his life – could be closed to him forever.

He felt sick to his stomach, and this time it wasn't the smell of chamber pots being dumped onto the street. The thing that had given his purpose and allowed him to provide for his family...gone.

His mouth was dry and Nigel felt like he was traversing though a desert. A moment ago, rivulets of sweat started falling down his head, now replacing with a flush face.

How was he going to take care of his siblings? His wife? Lovelace was already down on him; what would he do if he had to move? It would do no one any good if he were in a debtor's prison.

A carriage with rickety wheels on the cobblestones brought him out of his head. As it passed, Nigel's vision blurred; he thought he saw two carriages. Shaking his head, he kept going, until the street started spinning.

"Oh no," He said, leaning up against the closest gas lamppost. Closing his eyes, he stood straight, keeping his breathing steady. After a count of ten, he opened his eyes and the world was still again. Reginald walked toward him, and Nigel wasn't sure how much time had passed.

"I had no idea he was going to do that, Nigel. I didn't even get to present our case."

"It's not your fault, old chap."

"What are you going to do now?"

"I have to break the news to Ivy," Nigel said, "And figure out something before her father shames me into taking a position on the floor of his plant."

"If you need anything, you know where to find me."

"Thank you. Bring those killers in. And if you need Charles to help with any gadgets…"

"I'll let you know."

They shook hands.

Nigel remembered little of the walk home. He remembered opening the front door and ending up in the kitchen. Charles was there, and he had a large knife that was thrice the size of the cheese he was cutting.

"Ivy waits," Charles said, pointing to the ceiling.

"Thank you."

He didn't make much effort to quiet his steps, the footfalls echoing. He thought he heard Ivy call to him.

Nigel opened the door to his bedroom, which had the curtains drawn halfway, letting in slivers of light. The room was dark enough to hide everything from the bed up in shadow. A soft moan permeated the thick silence.

"Ivy?"

"Hello, darling. My corset is tight, and I can't get it off."

She whipped the covers off the bed, revealing her porcelain skin, bare except for her corset, which sat right over the middle of her bosom.

"Do you think you can help me?"

Ivy was brilliant at coming up with things like this to keep the relationship fresh, and any other time Nigel's body would be at war: his brain commending her ingenuity and his male organ excited for other obvious reasons.

Today, however, he couldn't muster a grin. Ivy sat up when she saw his face. "What is it?"

Nigel collapsed on the edge of the bed and told her the news, provoking a gasp and a hug. "Darling, I am *so* sorry."

"He even had the gall to threaten Reginald with the same fate if he brought me on as a consultant."

"A wise play," Ivy said. "A little too wise for your chief. Even on his best day, he'd never win prizes for his intellect."

"All the more reason to suspect Rushforth's hand in this."

"Proving it has gotten harder."

"That's one way to look at it," Nigel said, which made Ivy glance his way. "Another would be to see I am free to pursue my instincts."

"Nigel, you just said Willoughby warned you-"

"Against using police protocols. I have other methods to employ."

"Never knew you had a shadowy side, husband."

"I am full of surprises. It's time Rushforth found out as well."

***

Nigel found Lord Bellamy in the kitchen with Charles when he descended the stairs. Bellamy smiled and stood when he made eye contact.

"Good afternoon, Nigel."

"Lord Bellamy, welcome. I trust Charles has played a suitable host?"

"Quite so. Today I am here to call on Minnie. I have tickets to the flower show at Piccadilly Circus."

"I'm sure that will be lovely."

"That is my hope." Bellamy adjusted his cufflinks. "I don't suppose you could help a fellow man in need, and tell me her favorite?"

"I am afraid I must disappoint you. While I know my sister well, that is not something we share."

The corners of Bellamy's mouth creased downward for a moment.

"Fear not, she isn't shy about saying what suits her."

"Then it falls on my ears to be open."

Their conversation quieted when Minnie and Ivy came down, laughing. Minnie wore a blue satin gown with cream fringe. Her gloves and hat were cream. Ivy wore a simple pink gown, proper for a chaperone but still elegant for a young married woman.

Bellamy bowed. "Minnie, Mrs. Barrington, you look lovely."

"But not too lovely", Nigel said, which caused Ivy to shoot him daggers. "Minnie has threatened to adopt a more liberal wardrobe. Was all an effort to raise my pulse. That's enough of me talking. Enjoy yourselves."

Nigel's unwavering concentration on strategizing against Rushforth left him unaware of their departure, failing to even offer a wave goodbye.

CHAPTER 12

Charles was knee-deep in experiments when Nigel came down the next morning. He knelt in front of a beaker with a light green liquid. It was brighter than anything Nigel recalled hearing about, or reading in those fantastical fiction novels, like the ones that Jules Verne wrote.

"Good morning, brother," Nigel said. "How goes your work?"

"Phosphorous," Charles said.

"Of course," Nigel said, clearing his throat. Despite his brother's simple nature, he had a marvelous command of science.

"Not enough," Charles continued.

"You will get it before long," Nigel said. "I'm wondering if I might borrow your duster this morning. Got to head out into the cold, and I recall you saying how warm it is."

Charles didn't answer, moving closer to the beaker filled with green liquid. Nigel watched it for a moment, and he could've sworn it got brighter.

"Is that safe, Charles?"

Charles pointed at his brother's chest. Nigel straightened, then turned around. Charles had been pointing to his wardrobe. Even though he required care for the rest of his life, Charles was smarter and some ways more empathetic than most people.

Nigel smiled and opened the wardrobe. A few items of clothing that were stuffed in there fell out toward him. He tried to grab them all, but some hit the ground. Nigel chuckled as he picked them up. Charles had had the same wardrobe since he was a child. While it was certainly tall enough to accommodate his adult frame, it wasn't deep inside. He rifled through the clothes, sometimes coming across sacks containing rolled up parchment. *No doubt notes Charles kept on his various experiments.*

Nigel rifled through the clothes, marveling at the fact that some of them looked like others had never worn them. Nigel speculated that the rest might have been forgotten donations for those souls in the workhouses. He found the duster on the far right and pulled it out. Nigel surmised it was big enough to fit him and Charles. He took it off the hanger, only to realize the left shoulder had a hole in it. Nigel let out a soft growl of annoyance, but pushed that thought down. *What is the expression? Beggars cannot be choosers.*

He gave it another look and put it on. He nodded, recognizing that it would enable him to seamlessly blend in with the areas he was heading towards. And, if he got too close to Rushforth, he could take it off. Nigel hoped it wouldn't go that far.

"Thank you, Charles. And good luck with your experiments."

He walked upstairs, pausing halfway up. He turned back to his brother, who got closer to the beaker on his desk.

"If you get a chance," Nigel said, "Please look in on Ivy. Maybe ask her to make you some tea. I think she could use the company today."

"Sister and I talk," Charles said. "She likes stories."

Nigel raised an eyebrow. "Oh? Stories about what?"

"Baby Nigel. Short pants and silly dance."

Nigel laughed and shook his head. "Whatever works, Shakespeare. Good day, brother."

Ivy was buttering toast when Nigel came upstairs. She smiled at him. "Good morning, beloved," she said, eyeing the duster. "Do you have an audience with the Queen this morning?"

"Of a sort," Nigel said. "It'll do no good to keep tabs on Rushforth if he knows I am following him."

Ivy glowered at him, dropping the knife on purpose. "Nigel Barrington, you agreed to discuss what we're going to do about your predicament, which involves you getting too close to these aristocrats."

"I most definitely did," Nigel replied. "But I didn't agree to doing it first thing. And I have limited time to catch Rushforth at his morning meetings."

"Are you sure he's even involved?"

"I *know* it's a gamble to go after Rushforth. Every setback I've incurred since I caught Spring-Heeled Jack, Rushforth has been around. He's tied to this. I know it."

"That doesn't explain the ghastly murders of those young women. You think Rushforth is the killer?"

"I cannot prove that yet, but I am banking on him leading me to someone who is. The cuts on those girls – a surgeon could do that. He will know them."

He turned to face her. "I will solve this. It's just a matter of time."

"I admire your convictions, dear, but that's taking an awful chance, is it not? I mean, if Rushforth sees you-"

"That's the beauty of it, my love." Nigel said, daring to step closer, despite Ivy holding sharp cutlery in her hand. "He spends every morning at Wessex Down." He smiled, baring his teeth. "He's the patron of their chef, and his picture is above the mantle. Lord Rushforth is their most important customer."

"It is to your advantage that you're so handsome when you talk like that," Ivy said. "But you must do me a favor."

"Anything."

"Do not find yourself in jail."

"I swear on the lives of my siblings."

"Nigel, you shouldn't do that!"

"I agree, darling, but I needed to convey I understand the severity of my predicament."

Ivy nodded, then gestured for him to come to her. He pressed his lips against hers, wrapping his arms around her hips. She giggled softly in delight.

Nigel pulled away and put the duster on. "Wish me luck and please relay to Minnie that we will discuss her staying out all night later."

Ivy opened her mouth to speak, but before she could, Nigel continued. "That means ALL of us."

Ivy watched him go and nibbled on the buttered toast. "This will be quite the day," she said.

***

"For a place with its reputation," Nigel muttered to himself, "Wessex Down doesn't look like much."

Nestled near the corner of Portland Place, Wessex Down looked more like an office of a doctor or dentist on Baker Street - darker colors on the exterior walls. A sign with gold on the edges that lost its luster, and paint that had faded so much you couldn't read it from more than a few paces away.

When Nigel walked inside, he saw a much different view: pristine marble tables, impeccably polished silverware, and the finest china.

He watched as the diners took careful bites, closing their eyes as they savored their food.

Nigel snorted. As he inhaled again, his nose was tempted with the scent of roasted duck, chicken, and foie gras, molded into little balls. Nigel had heard his mother-in-law speak of it, calling it a ballette.

"Are you waiting on a guest, sir?" The maitre d' asked, hands clasped in front of him. A young man – he guessed he was around Minnie's age – twenty-two – he smiled, his eyes wide and his smile inviting. He was eager to serve, no doubt because of the clientele.

"Just one this morning," Nigel said. The maitre d' nodded, and grabbed a bound, leather menu, gesturing for Nigel to follow.

Nigel's eyes darted back and forth, on the lookout for Rushforth. His intel, which he reviewed in the carriage ride over, revealed that the aristocrat took brunch meetings in Wessex Down three days a week. The notes specified little about his fellow diners, other than 'they were of similar dress and prominence'.

Rushforth was not seated anywhere along the path to his table. But Nigel's disappointment was short-lived, as the maitre d' pointed to a table where Nigel could sit with his back against the wall and watch the entire restaurant.

Nigel accepted the menu from the maitre d', who poured him a cup of tea before returning to his post. Nigel sipped the tea and opened the menu.

His eyes widened at the prices of the items – something as simple as a biscuit, sausage and tea was almost one-third his weekly salary. "Must be one hell of a biscuit," Nigel whispered.

"Good morning, sir."

Nigel looked up to see the waiter standing at the far end of his table. His beard, came down to his collar. He had bags under his eyes and rough hands, but he was pleasant and his smile inviting.

"Are you prepared to hear today's specials?" he asked.

I've no doubt they are wonderful," Nigel said, "But I'm a simple man. A sausage, biscuit and tea will be sufficient."

The waiter nodded. "Very well, sir."

Nigel swallowed hard, then sipped more tea. *Ivy would understand. Wouldn't she?*

Laughter filled the room as Lord Rushforth walked in, flanked by three men. Nigel shuffled in his seat as they walked toward him.

Nigel blinked as the men took their seats. While Rushforth dressed in a Savile Row suit – dark green suit, a waistcoat with bright yellow flowers on it – the rest of the men dressed like Nigel.

"What in the Queen's name are you up to?" Nigel whispered aloud. He sipped his tea as the men sat and gave the order to the waiter, who had rushed over as they sat down.

Rushforth sat facing Nigel's seat, which caused the former police detective to choke on his tea. It burned going down, and he turned away from them, putting his hand against his mouth. He felt his throat spasm and a cough erupted out, but with the surrounding laughter, Rushforth ignored it.

Nigel gestured for the waiter, who came over right away. "Might I have some more tea? And could I see the menu again? Seeing all of this amazing food made me realize I might be hungrier than I thought."

"Right away, sir," the waiter said. He turned around and grabbed a menu from his colleague. Nigel took it and held up in front of his face, covering everything below his eyes.

Rushforth's audience was hanging on his every word. He couldn't discern the subject, but the men were rapt.

The waiter and his flowery teapot interrupted the reconnaissance, forcing Nigel to lower his menu. He tried to compensate by leaning back in his chair, hoping the small pockets of darkness creeping in from the window could hide him.

"Have you decided on anything else, sir?"

"Not yet," Nigel said. "I need some more time."

The waiter bowed and walked away, allowing Nigel to use the menu once again as camouflage. He eyed Rushforth and the cronies, leaning his ear toward them, but heard little more than before.

Nigel closed his eyes, taking a deep breath. He counted his breaths for about ten seconds, then focused on the patrons. He recognized some older men and women speaking in soft tones. Nigel also listened to a mother instruct her daughter on the proper way to fold her napkin.

His ear twitched as he caught a deep laugh, followed by a "Right you are, my good man."

There you are, Lord Rushforth.

The conversation continued, mostly Rushforth talking. "Our latest ventures look promising," he said, and the men murmured among themselves. "Once the next phase is complete, we will purchase the businesses in question."

Nigel opened his eyes. "Next phase, eh?"

The waiter came with the meal. "Thank you, young man. I think I had a momentary weakness. This meal looks filling enough," Nigel said, returning the menu.

The waiter bowed and walked away. Nigel took a bite of the sausage, chewing it with delight. The spice and heat were just perfect. It was juicy, each bite tasting savory. He smiled, feeling better about spending so much on lunch.

Rushforth and his hangers-on ate in silence the rest of the meal, which Nigel didn't mind. He savored each bite, and when he finished, his exhale was just as much lamenting its end as signifying he was full.

Rushforth said something with a sneer grin, and stood, his lunch-mates' laughter a loud roar in the restaurant. Some diners, mainly women, gasped or sneered in Rushforth's direction. Two men, presumably married to the offended women, stared daggers or pointed, signaling the end of the protest.

Nigel dabbed the corners of his mouth with his napkin, and stood, bumping the edge of the table. It sounded like it echoed in the restaurant, exacerbated by people giving him rude looks. He cursed under his breath and bent forward. Nigel looked up, swallowing hard as the man at the end of Rushforth's party turned toward him.

Nigel jerked his head forward, his hat falling off his head. He bent down on one knee and took a few deep breaths, trying to not only slow his racing heartbeat, but give Rushforth's men a wide berth.

Two more deep breaths, and Nigel no longer felt his heart pounding against his chest. He stood, putting his hat on, and walking toward the door. He reached into his pocket, grabbing some money, and plucking it down at the maitre d's table.

"Fine service to accompany your most excellent meal," Nigel said bowing. The maitre d responded by raising his nose.

Nigel popped the door open and poked his head out, making sure Rushforth and his friends weren't right outside. He spotted them across the street, Rushforth's stovepipe hat sticking out above the heads of his compatriots. They stopped at the corner store across the street, discussing whatever they saw in the window.

Nigel moved toward them, keeping his eyes on Rushforth. He didn't hear the wheels of the oncoming carriage and neighing horse until it was within six feet of him. He backed up, ignoring the unintelligible ranting of the cockney carriage driver as it moved past. Nigel looked at the corner store, but no one was there.

Making sure no other carriages were in his way, Nigel ran to the store. The cobblestones in front of the store continued past it in the shape of an 'L', and Nigel smiled as he ran toward it. He was still moving unseen.

Shadows danced on the brick wall opposite the corner store, getting smaller as Nigel got closer. He stopped at the corner of the L, taking a moment to catch his breath. Poking his head out, Nigel saw Rushforth's hat get smaller as he traversed the alley, his men in tow.

Nigel continued toward his target, moving as fast as he could without running. A couple came toward him, the woman twirling a parasol. Nigel deftly moved to her left, focused on Rushforth's white hat.

The group slowed as the alley opened into another street, and the party turned left. Nigel kept his pace and was soon in the wide street, at least two dozen people milling about. Nigel couldn't see Rushforth, and he brushed past two men aside so he could pass, ignoring their demands for apology. Rushforth stopped and turned his head in Nigel's direction.

"Blimey," he said, shortening his footsteps. His calves ached at the sudden change in muscle motion. *These stiff oxford shoes don't help matters.*

Nigel spotted two men, faces covered in grime, wearing aprons and chatting in Gaelic. He walked up to them.

"Gentlemen," he said, tipping his cap. "Just pausing here. Don't mind me."

"A bheil thu craicte?" The taller, bearded one said.

"Faigh a-mach as a silk," the smaller one said, spittle flying from his mouth, "A wanker filth!"

Nigel looked over the shorter man's bowler hat, as Rushforth shook the hand of a man in a plaid suit, who left their group and walked into a warehouse at the end of the block.

"Good day to you too," Nigel said, walking past, confident nothing the men said was a friendly greeting.

Rushforth and the remaining members moved on, slowing their pace. Nigel smiled, picking up his pace, doubling the length of his stride. The white stovepipe hat moved a few paces, then stopped, repeating this twice.

Keeping his eye on Rushforth's group, and mindful of couples and young ones moving about around him, Nigel found himself at the end of the block. He did a double take at the building. A fading wooden sign atop the door proclaimed it *as "Bradley & Sons, Purveyors of Fine Woodwork."*

Nigel sidestepped to the window and looked inside. Sure enough, men inside moved wood, shaping it into chairs, benches, and bed-posts.

"What in Babbage's name?" he said to himself, stepping back to carry on after Rushforth.

Nigel jogged across the street, only to find Rushforth alone with one man, a newsboy's cap in hand, running meaty fingers through greasy hair. Rushforth chuckled and looked to Nigel, who froze in place.

Rushforth's newsboy capped companion stepped forward, putting his foot atop the bottom step of a small staircase. He obstructed Rushforth's view of Nigel, who took advantage of the opportunity to turn around and face a glass wall. It was a bakery, fresh bread in the window, steam rising. Nigel used the glass to see Rushforth wave as his friend ascended the stairs into "Mallory Finance, Inc."

Nigel waited until he was out of Rushforth's peripheral vision and ran to the door of the finance company. And just like at Bradley's, men were engaged in the business that was advertised on the door.

Are these fronts? Is Rushforth perhaps trying to hide his evil acts in plain sight? But if so, why go to such considerable expense to make it look legitimate? Most people were oblivious to things like that unless they needed these companies' services.

No, it couldn't be, Nigel thought to himself. Rushforth doesn't think too highly of those under his boot. He would flaunt it, daring Nigel and his – former – police colleagues to come after him.

He heard a man yell out, and a carriage stop fifteen paces in front of him. The driver descended the hansom and opened the door for Rushforth, who entered and promptly closed the curtains. Nigel watched as the cab sped off, his biggest hunch a total dud.

CHAPTER 13

Nigel stood there in the street, mulling his next move, until a carriage driver cried and snapped the reins of his horses, and Nigel hurried off the street.

"This is right cocked up," Nigel whispered to himself. Was Rushforth just another stuffy nobleman who thought himself better than the rank and file? Did he pander to men of industry, stringing them along for the attention they provided?

This thought process dissipated when he found himself in front of Mallory Finance.

From what Nigel knew of business, it was prudent to minimize expenses as much as possible. And Mallory certainly did that: only three desks were in the room, spaced about twenty-five to thirty feet apart. Each desk had a bank ledger, quill, and ink.

And despite watching someone enter, it surprised Nigel to see the room devoid of people.

He looked right, his ears turned toward the rear of the room. Nigel held his breath for five heartbeats, trying to focus his hearing.

"Not a sound," Nigel whispered as he exhaled. He smiled. *This is more like what I expected.*

He walked, keeping his steps measured. Nigel wasn't sure why he moved that way, other than habit. No one was here, right?

But he knew Newsboy Cap walked in here, and if Rushforth had seen him and warned him, then it remained prudent to be ready.

There were no papers on the desks. There wasn't *anything*, for that matter, and nothing was out of place.

No one is that *neat. Especially in London.*

He straightened, reaching the back wall. From the front, it looked like just that: a wall. As Nigel inspected it closer, he saw a white line – a rectangle – on it. A door.

Nigel put his left hand into his coat and pushed his fingers against the hidden door. He sighed, just realizing he didn't arm himself with his knife.

His fingertips reddened as he pressed the "invisible" door and opened. He expected to find someone up to some nefarious activity. Instead, Nigel was in a narrow hallway, barely wide enough to accommodate him and his wife.

Stepping forward, he waited for an echo, but Nigel was relieved to discover there wasn't one. He kept the door open behind him, so he could see without looking for a candle. Walking down the corridor, Nigel kept his fingers on the wall, in case he discovered another secret hideaway.

The room looked much longer than it was, but Nigel was sure his long steps cut the travel time down. There were no other secret passages or offices.

The room opened into a back alley. Nigel stepped forward, eyes darting left and right. Newsboy Cap was rather large, and Nigel didn't want to be surprised if he attacked.

He continued on to a dock, walking to the edge of the wooden planks. It wasn't very wide, just enough for a two-man canoe or rowboat.

Removing his hat, Nigel scratched his head. Where did this dock go? It was obvious it was a perk of having the office and would take the boatmen to a larger dock or boat. Without taking a swim in the muddy Thames, there was no way to determine how far it went.

He knelt, looking for any marks or signs that Newsboy Cap was there. He couldn't see anything and groaned in frustration. Putting his hat down, he looked underneath the wooden planks. With the clouds obscuring the sun, his search was for naught.

Nigel sat up on his knees. The dock here was strange, more a novelty of those with money, rather than out of place. He had hoped there'd be something here, but Lady Luck was not on his side.

He bent down to push himself up off his knees, and out of the corner of his eye, detected movement.

To his left, something was flapping in the breeze. He reached out and pulled a small piece of fabric that was lodged on a windowsill. In this light- or lack thereof – he couldn't tell if it was dark red or purple. The edges were frayed, something the size of a button on it. Nigel removed his gloves and touched it. It was dried and caked on. Could it be blood? It had seeped in too much to tell.

Nigel smiled. *Charles, I wonder if one of your lights can expose its secrets.*

He looked up and smiled, a gesture of thanks to the Almighty. Pocketing the fabric and putting his hat on, Nigel took deliberate steps back into the hallway.

***

Nigel found an empty carriage and negotiated a ride home. At this time of day, the early shift would start letting out soon, and it was better if he avoided being seen, especially given what he found.

He closed the curtain to his left. He shut the one to his right, but left it open enough to allow some light in and took out the fabric. In the pale light, Nigel could tell it was red, faded enough to make it look purple. He turned it over in his hands and saw the spot where the stain embedded itself. It was dark, almost a perfect circle. He sniffed it, but there was no discernible smell. Nigel's experience told him that, given where he found it, the stain was likely one of three things: blood, dirt or grease. Determining that would have to wait. *There's no chance of me getting into the police labs. Not without assistance, but I'd have to give someone a reason to trust me.*

Nigel went down to the lab, but Charles was asleep. He did not know what equipment his brother had down here. It was never good to wake up Charles, because he got cranky and took time to calm down. He couldn't afford that right now.

He sighed. "Looks like I'm making an appointment to see Winifred."

***

"I assure you, Officer Barrington-"

"Inspector," Nigel corrected. *Sure, I'm suspended, but you can at least use my correct title.*

Winifred bowed. "*Inspector* Barrington, that Minnie's dress will be the height of fashion at a price agreeable to your budget."

"While I appreciate that," Nigel said, tipping his cap. "It's not why I am here."

"Oh?" Winifred asked, a mischievous grin on her face.

"I'm hoping you might tell me more about this," Nigel continued, producing the small piece of fabric from his coat pocket.

Winifred took it, rubbing it in her hand. She moved to the counter and opened a drawer, pulling out a small cylindrical device that she held up to her eye.

"I am not questioning the methods of a professional," Nigel said, "But I am curious to know what that is?"

"It's a jeweler's loupe. My brother gave it to me. I've had issues with knockoff fabrics on some of my orders, and I use this to determine what's real or not."

"Brilliant," Nigel said, backing away and gesturing for her to continue.

Winifred put the fabric on the counter and put the loupe over it. "Where did you get this little gem?" Winfred inquired, Nigel detecting her sarcastic tone.

"Found it in a pile of garbage," he said. Winifred looked up at him, eyebrow raised. "In my opinion, the color looks great on my beloved wife, and I'm curious if it's one of your creations."

Winifred put the loupe down and took the fabric in her hand. "I've never had a red this dark in my inventory – not that I couldn't get it for you.

"And *my* fabrics never allow a stain to set in," She continued, pointing to the dark dot. "What is that, anyway?"

"I do not know," Nigel replied. "Dirt would be my guess. Do you know who *would* have a fabric like that in stock?"

"Inspector, are you suggesting you'd purchase a dress elsewhere?"

"I'm just being thorough," Nigel replied with a wink. "If you have a swatch of something similar, I'll let Ivy choose which one she likes."

Winifred smiled and opened a drawer, holding up a small pile of swatches like cards in a poker game. She pulled out a lighter red, like the fan Minnie used in the summer.

"Takes all the fun out of the surprise that way," Winifred said, handing the swatch over, "But I appreciate the chance to continue earning your family's business."

"Obliged," Nigel said, pocketing the swatch and the original fabric, before putting his hat back on and walking to the door.

"If I were to guess," Winifred said as Nigel opened the door, "Wicker's Fine Fabrics might have a color like that."

"Thank you ever so much," Nigel said, bowing as he left.

CHAPTER 14

Wicker's Fine Fabrics wasn't that far from Winifred's establishment - about a ten-to-fifteen-minute walk – but Nigel used that time to think and not have to worry about bumping into people. He held the fabric up to the sun and it still looked red, but like Winifred said, it was dirty – probably had some mud on it. It could be red, or pink.

Old Mrs. Pemberton immediately came to his head.

He saw, in his mind's eye, her describing the bird demon, and the word pink. That replayed until the sound of a horse neighing in front of him brought him out of his reverie. Nigel jumped into the carriage, telling the driver of his destination.

Nigel sniffed the fabric, but got nothing specific, other than a musty smell, which made sense if it was on the ground anywhere in London.

The carriage stopped, the momentum carrying Nigel forward, forcing him to brace himself against the side walls. He put the fabric in his pocket, adjusted his coat and stepped out.

Wicker's was a generations-old business, or the outside wasn't as much of a priority as what went on inside. Dirt and ash formed a cake-like layer on the windowsill, similar to what one sees during a snowstorm. The sign faded so much you had to be within two meters to read it.

Nigel stepped inside and did a double take. Everything was pristine – immaculate floors, bright spools of fabric on the shelf behind the desks and sample dresses on hangars on either side of the main carpet.

A man came out to greet him. His suit looked new, as if he wore it for the first time. Not a stain on it, no stitch out of place. He had a thick moustache and a warm smile.

"Good afternoon, sir, I am Wicker, the proprietor. How may I assist you today?"

"Good afternoon, Mr. Wicker," Nigel said, pulling the piece of fabric from his pocket. "I'm told you might have this color in stock. Problem is, I'm not entirely sure what color it is."

He handed it to Wicker, who took it and looked it over. When he saw the dirt and mud, recoiled with mild disgust. "I can understand your confusion, sir. Where did you find this?"

"I couldn't say, as my sister brought it to me," Nigel explained, telling him about Minnie's upcoming societal debut.

"Ah," Wicker said as he put the fabric on the counter and produced a jeweler's loupe from a drawer behind him. He looked it over, murmuring to himself.

Nigel took this opportunity to look at the fabrics he *could* see, but there was no solid pink, just a white one with pink flowers on it, just like the description of the Bird Demons. *No way Mrs. Pemberton could see that much detail with those squinting eyes.*

Wicker opened another drawer and pulled out a very thick book. It reminded Nigel of drawings of the Gutenberg Bible that his father showed him as a child. Wicker opened it, revealing swatches of a variety of fabrics.

"Good heavens," Nigel proclaimed, "Is that every kind of fabric available in the world?"

"Were that so," Wicker said, smiling. "These are the Wicker offerings from the past three seasons. And," Wicker said, rifling through the book. "I don't think we offered that particular color."

He turned another page and was halfway through the book and pointed to a color near the bottom. He slid the book to Nigel. It was pink, albeit muted, and Nigel said as much.

"That is from last spring's collection, a favorite of debutantes in Chelsea," Wicker said. "It's faded, being in this book for over a year, but I'd guess if your sister was certain that...piece started as pink, this is all we had."

"So you don't offer it anymore? Even any extra pieces lying around?"

"We only sell a complete garment, sir," Wicker explained, "And we depleted our inventory this past winter during our holiday sale. It was peculiar, too, two women purchased the last two. I mentioned the upcharge to tailor it to them, and they didn't balk. It was a relief that they didn't need them for Christmas, considering the requested alterations.

"We pride ourselves on our ability to make any alteration to please our customers, sir. These young women also requested for leather petticoats."

"Really?"

"That's what I said. But I'm not one to pry into a customer's personal business. I figured it was for the cold, to keep them warm."

"I see," Nigel said, taking the piece of fabric back from Wicker. "You've been most helpful, sir. Thank you."

"If you can bring your sister in, we can look at-"

"I'm afraid she is very particular, Mr. Wicker, but we may just do that. Thank you." Nigel tipped his cap and left.

***

Nigel studied the fabric as he walked up the stairs to his house. He was so oblivious that he didn't see Ivy open the door just as he approached. Ivy smiled at him, turning into a frown as he walked by without acknowledging her.

She cleared her throat, and he stopped, eyes blinking as it registered where he was. Nigel shook his head, smiled and kissed Ivy on the cheek.

"Forgive me, my darling," Nigel said, relaying his story.

"That is quite interesting," Ivy replied. "What are you going to do now?"

"See what marvelous contraption Charles has that can help me analyze it."

"Minnie and I have lunch today with some of our friends. We'll see what we can find out."

Nigel shot her a look, but she lifted her hand in protest. "I know what you're going to say, my love, but it's just lunch. And with *this* group of ladies, we don't have to ask questions. They will offer the juicy gossip."

Nigel shook his head, chuckling. "Please be careful. I cannot bear the thought-"

She put her finger on his lips. "Then don't think it," Ivy said, kissing him. "Go see Charles, and Minnie and I will report back later."

***

He descended the stairs, looking around for Charles. Clanging brass on brass led him right to his brother, who was trying to join two large brass cylinders together.

"New project?"

"Make the old new," Charles said.

"A wonderful idea," Nigel said. "We don't have infinite resources in this world, after all."

Charles mumbled, his preferred method of agreement.

"I need your help," Nigel said, turning the fabric over in his hand. "Do you have anything that can analyze this?"

He held the fabric out. Charles kept at his brass cylinders, screwing bolts in with a heavy wrench.

"I must insist," Nigel continued, "A girl's life may depend on it. A girl like Minnie."

Charles dropped the wrench on the table, loud enough that Nigel winced. He didn't realize he was holding his breath until he saw his brother facing him, reaching for the fabric.

"Sis?" Charles asked.

"No," Nigel said, letting go of the fabric. "But someone like her, whose brother misses her."

Charles pulled the fabric close to his eye. Nigel smiled. The methods were unorthodox, but they got results.

"Supper time," Charles said.

"Not yet, Charles," Nigel said, looking at his pocket watch. "Did Minnie not give you a scone with tea?"

Charles shook his head and held up the fabric. "Supper."

Nigel shook his head. "Of course, you'll have answers at supper time. Splendid. Thank you, Charles."

He mumbled again and went back to his project. Nigel went upstairs to his wardrobe.

***

It wasn't much of a wardrobe; at least not what Nigel had seen at homes of more prominent citizens – including his father-in-law – but it served a purpose.

He opened it and removed the two pairs of shoes in the front to reveal a small box. Nigel opened it, revealing police files.

It was not a procedure for inspectors to take their work home, but it wasn't frowned upon either. And since his suspension, Nigel figured enough time had passed that his superiors would forget that he had them.

He sat in the chair, opening the first file, and perusing it. They consisted of notes from the inspectors and bobbies on the scene, along with some daguerreotype images.

The first folder had eyewitness reports of the Spring-Heeled Jack, which Nigel used to build a profile and hunt him down. *Wish I had the subsequent one right now.*

Nigel tossed that aside, and the papers spewed out onto the ground. He groaned and picked them up, crumbling some up along the way. Nigel took the folder and slammed it on the ground.

His heartbeat slowed, and he took stock of what he had done. *This isn't the conduct of a gentleman, to say nothing of a police inspector. Setbacks are part of the job, and life. Our reactions to the are what matter.*

Besides, that didn't change the fact that young women were being killed. They were at the start of their life. Some of them were moving up in station, others about to become mothers, and they were robbed of that chance. And those who were born to the right person, who had the favor of the Queen – or someone close to the monarch – got to tell the police they weren't allowed to pursue those victims' cases.

Nigel stood, adjusted his shirt and put the items back in the file. Taking a deep breath, he sat back down and pored through the third and final folder. Three quarters of it didn't relate to the investigation he spearheaded. Nigel told himself he'd read one more page before calling it quits.

He read the first paragraph, eyes widening. "Bingo," Nigel whispered. "This is it."

Nigel's finger danced among the words, describing the first missing woman and her clothes. It was a dress made of a muslin cotton fabric.

"It's in the report, so it must be important," Nigel said as he took a notebook from his pocket and jotted notes. He thanked God for this fortunate turn of events, returning the files to the shelf. Nigel thought he heard the front door open, and he made his way downstairs.

Ivy and Minnie were there, sharing a chuckle as they folded their coats. They turned to Nigel as his shoes clopped at the base of the stairs, smiling. It was eerie how similar their grins were, and Nigel commented as much.

"Is it so wrong that the women in your life are happy to see you?" Ivy asked, winking.

"Exactly," Minnie said. "Especially because I hear wives hate their husband after seven years of marriage."

Ivy snorted. She looked up at Nigel and held her arms up, as if to say she apologized.

"And how long do they say older brothers get annoyed at their bratty little sisters?"

Minnie stuck her tongue out in mock anger in response.

"Are you hungry, my dear?" Ivy asked.

"I'm feeling peckish," Nigel said.

"I'll get started. How does meat pie sound?"

"From your hands, my darling, heavenly," Nigel said, and meant it. With everything going on, he could use the distraction of a nice home-cooked meal with his family.

CHAPTER 15

Nigel took a bite of the meat pie, the spices filling his taste buds, the potatoes melting in his mouth. He closed his eyes, savoring the bite.

"Thank you," Ivy said, smiling.

"Was your day productive?" Minnie asked, wiping the corners of her mouth with a napkin. Nigel shared his findings and what Charles said he could do.

"And?" Ivy asked.

Nigel looked at his brother. "Charles?"

Charles looked up from his plate, eyes darting between Ivy and Nigel. "Still eating," he said.

Nigel emitted a quiet chuckle, shaking his head at his brother. What else could you do?

"We had quite the afternoon as well," Minnie said.

"That so? Please share," Nigel said, leaning forward.

"It was quite wonderful. They buttered the toast just right, and they made the tea not too hot. Though they were light on the sugar cubes. That was surprising."

"Brevity is the soul of wit, Minnie," Nigel said. "And I do have pressing matters to attend to."

"You remember my friend Martha, right?" Ivy asked, prompting a nod from Nigel. "She helps her husband's cleaning business when the lad is ill or they take double-book jobs.

"One of them is at a money-lending house. Normally, it's a routine cleaning job, that she can get done in an hour or two. And she said that normally it's not something she'd comment on."

"Except for two things," Minnie added. She looked at Ivy, who nodded for her to continue. "The first, is that she was asked to clean during the day, *and no one is ever there.*"

Nigel leaned forward, elbows on the table, fingers steepled together. The women had his attention.

"And there was one man she saw around the office, but he was near the entrance or walking away from it."

"Never inside," Ivy added.

"Precisely. She described him as rather rotund, wearing a cap like her newsboy nephew."

Nigel's eyes widened. "A newsboy cap? You're sure?"

"Yes, she was quite adamant that he looked juvenile," Minnie said.

"Despite his girth," Ivy said.

"Despite his girth," Minnie repeated.

He shook off their repetitive statements – *I'm glad they're close, but my word* – and stood up. *This sounds like the empty money-changing house I investigated earlier. And it seems my rather rotund friend likes to hang out at an empty establishment. Rather interesting.*

"Ivy, dinner was magnificent, thank you. I will clean up tonight if you'll allow Charles to show me what he found."

Charles looked up, chewing the last bite of food. He opened his mouth to speak.

"You're done. You ate it all. Out with it."

Charles adjusted the tools on his desk, so they were in neat rows. He moved two small boxes above them in the left corner, ensuring their neatness as well. Nigel stifled the urge to goad his brother to speed up. Charles did things on his time, no matter the urgency. Nigel's patience knew no bounds as he fulfilled his duty to his brother.

Charles took a small handkerchief from his pocket and laid it out on his bench, smoothing out the wrinkles. Nigel watched as he walked over to his microscope and pulled out the red fabric, cupping it as if he were holding an animal or a child.

He laid the fabric down on the handkerchief, right in the middle. Leaning forward and closing his left eye, Charles pointing to the fabric and turned it over. Standing upright again, he nodded.

"What do we have here?" Nigel asked.

"Red dress," Charles said. "Blood."

Charles pointed to the circle on the fabric and Nigel nodded. *I knew it.*

"Water," Charles said. "Gross. Thames."

Nigel blinked at this statement. He watched Charles cup the fabric again and put it back under the microscope. Nigel walked over to the device as Charles, adjusting the objective lens right above the fabric.

Stepping forward, Nigel looked through the ocular lens. He saw a similar stain pattern on the edges of the fabric, right in front of the tear. This one was brown.

"My word," Nigel whispered. "I need to show this to Reginald."

He stepped back and squeezed his brother's shoulder. "This is very helpful, Charles. Thank you."

He headed for the stairs. "Memory!" Charles yelled, stopping Nigel in his tracks.

Charles held the fabric in his hands as if it were the most precious thing in the world. Nigel walked over and used both hands to take it.

"What would I do without you, Charles?"

"Suffer," Charles replied, earning a chuckle out of Nigel, who left his brother to his innocent machinations.

***

"Are you mad?" Reginald said, the teaspoon hitting the table and clanging, drawing attention from the other patrons. Nigel raised his arm at the wrist, and Reginald took a deep breath, then picked up his tea and sipped.

"I have the evidence," Nigel said, pulling a wrapped cloth from the interior breast pocket of his coat.

"There's no suspect or motive yet," he said, and pointed at Nigel. "And don't say it. You know we don't have all the equipment your brother has, and no way will Rushforth commission its use to confirm it."

"I am well aware of that," Nigel said, sipping his drink, "But it's more information than you have now. You've got good lads working for you. They can gather something you can take to our chief."

Reginald sighed. "I know you're trying to help. Believe me, I want to take this in. Pressure is coming from Her Majesty and Willoughby is feeling it, and us, too, as a result. This has to be *ironclad*. I don't know that we have enough yet.

"And besides," Reginald said as he sipped tea, "You are a better detective than I am. Without providing...*details* into how I conducted this investigation, questions could arise."

"Just know it's here. I'll still work on my end, as well. Let's hope the chief will take the evidence and see reason."

"A folly, that may be," Reginald said. "By the way, there are more reports of those Bird Demons."

"Let me guess, the same black outfits with hints of pink?"

Reginald sat back in his chair. "Why, yes."

"Thought so," Nigel said, sharing what he found at the dressmakers.

"Willoughby is going to be buggered about that," Reginald said. "You're supposed to be on top of that."

"I was demoted, remember?" Nigel said, taking out a folded piece of paper and opening it up.

"What's that?"

"Police report on the demons," Nigel said. "I took the liberty of filling it out for you. Maybe you can turn it in for me?"

"Right-o, old chap," Reginald said looking it over. "Well done. Be safe out there, my friend. Not only for me, but Ivy as well."

"I will," Nigel said, firmly believing it, despite the growing sense of dread welling up inside him.

CHAPTER 16

The flow of carriage traffic seemed to be more congested today, in Nigel's mind. He leaned against a wall as he counted eleven go by in the span of five minutes. *The wheels of progress never stop turning.*

Only after the last one passed by - a yellow carriage that made him do a double take – did Nigel move to the money lending house Newsboy Cap entered days before.

He felt his arm tense as he gripped the door handle. It creaked as he stepped inside, so he paused four heartbeats before moving on.

Making sure the door locked behind him, Nigel walked as quietly as he could.

It came as little surprise that he was once again alone. He perused them for evidence. Just like before, they had none.

"Just a front," Nigel said aloud, "But for what?"

A *whump* behind him made his ears wiggle and he turned toward it, leaning in the sound's direction. He detected a muffled voice yelling and headed for it. Nigel balled his fists, just in case.

He moved to the long corridor, where he met no resistance, and continued to the back door, and heard a voice that sounded like yelling, despite being muffled through the wall. Nigel kept going, willing his legs to walk as fast as they could go without running.

He stopped at the door, propping himself against the wall by the handle. He counted to five, exhaling slowly to calm his heart, beating more rapidly than he'd like. The muffled voice was softer now, as if it was moving away from Nigel.

Leaning closer to the door, Nigel tried to listen, but heard nothing. He looked down as he put his ear into the wall and saw his overcoat.

"I wore this before," Nigel said to himself. He turned his coat inside out and put it on, the white lining sticking out.

Something dropped out of the coat and hit the ground. Nigel knelt and picked it up. It was his goggles. He took off his hat and put them on.

"Right then," he said. He took a deep breath, opened the door and stood in the hallway.

The man in the newsboy cap turned to him, holding a rope that belonged to the rowboat at the dock. The fat man's mouth was agape.

Nigel punched him in the nose.

Newsboy Cap's head snapped back, but he adjusted and dropped the rope. He charged at Nigel, growling as he raised his fists. He feinted a right hook and jabbed with his left hand, connecting with Nigel's jaw.

He stumbled back against the wall, lifting his arms to prepare for a further attack, but none came. Instead, Nigel saw his opponent through the door at the end of the hallway, getting in a rowboat, knife in hand.

As Newsboy Cap cut the rope and sat down, Nigel stood, gripping the oars, pulling away from the dock. With his eyes fixed on his opponent, Nigel sprinted to the edge of the dock, causing his opponent's eyes to narrow and then widen in realization to what was about to happen.

Nigel leapt in the air.

He fell right into Newsboy Cap, who let go of the oars to catch his attacker. They hit the wooden floor and Nigel tried to put his forearm to his opponent's throat. A large layer of fat prevented Nigel from clamping down on his airway. Newsboy Cap punched Nigel in the ribs, and he rolled off, trying to catch his breath.

A shadow enveloped him, and Nigel saw his opponent standing over him, knife in hand.

He kicked Newsboy Cap in the knee. The man groaned and his legs buckled, then Nigel grabbed the man's wrist and twisted. The knife fell out of Newsboy Cap's fat hands and into Nigel's gloved palm. He swung it at Newsboy Cap, but the larger man was falling, and it grazed his clavicle.

Newsboy Cap regained his balance and pushed Nigel, who stumbled, off the boat and into the water. His hat fell off his head, but more urgent than that was the speed at which Nigel sank. His coat and pants were a heavier material and weighed him down.

Flapping his arms as fast as he could, he broke water and took a deep breath. He saw Newsboy Cap getting away. Nigel took two strokes forward but felt himself sinking. He looked back and saw the dock was close, so Nigel turned and swam toward it. When he reached the post, Newsboy Cap and his boat were long gone.

***

Nigel sat there until his breathing slowed and he felt centered. It took him approximately five minutes to get up, adjust his coat, and tightly put on his gloves.

He turned and headed back to Mallory's. His ear twitched as a loud echo filled the air, and Nigel realized his footsteps were making loud noises.

Hard to get the drop on my opponent and his cronies coming in like a clopping horse. He paused, taking three deep breaths before moving on, slowing his footsteps.

He was at Mallory's before he knew it, but he walked across the street first, so he could see that no one was waiting for him. Three carriages were converging on the road in front of the money house, and Nigel let them pass. He was in no rush, especially if trouble awaited.

He waited until the last one was gone before going inside.

When Nigel entered, he found a silent and clean office. "This is right mad," Nigel whispered. He took a few steps, deliberately lifting his foot higher than normal to muffle the sound. He paused for three heartbeats, then continued to the base of the stairs. Still no sound.

Nigel huffed and walked to the front door, opening it carefully and descending the stairs onto the street. He looked up, eyes widening as he looked across the street.

Ainsworth and two lackeys walked toward him, engaged in conversation.

Nigel froze. "Blimey."

CHAPTER 17

Nigel turned around, intending to walk away from Mallory's and Ainsworth. Instead, he wobbled on both legs, feeling his quad muscles tighten. He strained to move but couldn't.

Ainsworth's hearty guffaw was loud, letting Nigel knew the aristocrat was closing in.

Nigel straightened his back and walked, hoping he didn't draw attention to himself. He heard Ainsworth mumble to his companions, paying Nigel no mind as he walked past Mallory's. Ainsworth wiped his hand with a cloth and moved to put it in his pocket but missed and it hit the ground as he moved on, not paying attention.

Nigel moved to pick the cloth up, which had Ainsworth's crest of a knight in front of a flower.

Nigel pocketed it and walked away, exhaling in relief as he got as far from Mallory's as he could.

***

"I have a message for you, sir," the young lad, whose features were as polished and green as his uniform.

"Go ahead, son, out with it," Reginald said, equal parts amused and annoyed.

"Well, sir, uh, there's someone here to see you."

Reginald checked his watch. "I've got five minutes. Send him in," he said, returning to the paperwork on his desk.

The boy opened his mouth to speak, but only a faint hum left his vocal chords. Reginald sighed and dropped the paperwork, folding his hands together on his desk.

"He told me to tell you the circumstances," he said, recalling from memory, "Prevent his entrance here, but if you go to the pub next to where you got Mr. S.H. Jack, that would be lovely and first drink is on him."

Reginald's eyes grew wide and he was on his feet so fast, the Bobbie stepped back and ran into the door. "Inform the captain he'll have to wait," Reginald said, moving past the boy and forcing his legs to slow down so he wasn't running out of the station.

***

The Filthy Pirate, despite its name, was one of the cleaner drinking establishments that Reginald had visited. While it was in the opposite direction of his home, Reginald didn't mind joining some boys after a shift.

The décor was great as well – finely crafted wood made from old ships and nautical themed decorations adorned the place. Reginald liked to take time to look at them, but he was late for a meeting.

Instead, he made a beeline to the back of the bar, where he saw Nigel, hat on the table and his jacket turned inside out. Reginald raised an eyebrow at this, and Nigel looked down, chuckled, and took his jacket off, turning it right side out.

"Mighty brave of you to go to the station to ask me to come here," Reginald said.

"My disguise threw people off," Nigel replied, showing the interior of his coat. "New bobbies don't hurt, either."

"Must have something good."

Nigel looked past Reginald, and around the rest of the bar, before reaching into his pocket and pulling out a file that he folded in half. He slid it across the table to Reginald, using the cover of his top hat to keep it hidden.

Reginald looked to his right before opening the folder.

Nigel sat back in his seat, alternating his look between the pub and Reginald.

"Once a detective, always a detective, eh?" Reginald asked.

Nigel didn't speak because Reginald already knew the answer. He filled his friend in on Newsboy Cap and Lord Ainsworth's meetings.

"Nigel, he's a bloody aristocrat for Heaven's Sake," Reginald replied, not looking up from the folder.

"Newsboy isn't, and neither is the empty office."

"The elite among us are eccentric at best," Reginald said.

"If anyone knows the young women who died, it would be men from the aristocracy. Debutantes aren't commoners," Nigel reminded him.

"We also can't question them directly," Reginald replied, looking up from the paper. "Hence your current predicament. I appreciate why you picked this spot, Nigel, if I'm seen working with you..."

"I'm just a concerned citizen providing a tip."

Reginald sat back, smiling. "I could work with this, but I'm going to need a bit of time to make it look, how shall I say, more haphazard."

"More young women could die in the meantime."

"I can't even question the nobles involved, and some of them are very close to the deceased. Your Jack friend might give us something, but I can't touch him."

Nigel opened his mouth to retort, but Reginald raised a hand, stopping him.

"I've got more on the line than you," Reginald said. "My wife, children. You're young, as yet without children and you have a father-in-law who will take you in just to be proven right. It's not ideal, but *you* have options."

Nigel balled his fist and immediately let up. Reginald was his friend, yes, and Willoughby put him in a precarious position, but his unwillingness to stir up dust in order solve a case – and prevent further crimes – was frustrating. Sure, Reginald risked his job by coming to Nigel for help, but there was enough evidence to at least continue the line of inquiry. This inaction was causing fits.

"You have one, Reginald. Solve the bloody case."

"Willoughby has clarified that the noble's case is the one I have to solve."

"I'm not dropping this, Reginald," Nigel said, his eyes boring into Reginald. "The girls deserve justice."

A pregnant pause hung between them.

"Yes they do," Reginald agreed, taking a deep breath. "Give me fourteen hours. Need a way to place this."

Nigel nodded. "If I find anything else, I'll let you know."

"The sooner, the better," Reginald said. "Willoughby has his card game tomorrow. Might be in good spirits if he wins."

"Maybe I'll have to work on his fellow players."

"Be careful if you do," Reginald said, standing up. "Otherwise, your sister and wife might find herself a royal flush away from a new home."

Nigel frowned, but let out a laugh as Reginald winked and tipped his cap before he left. Nigel counted to ten once Reginald left the bar, paid his bill and walked out.

CHAPTER 18

Nigel smiled at the lanterns in the front window of the Skinner's house on the corner. It was a silly thing, putting the lanterns there, as no one sat in the front room – Mrs. Skinner had complained to him during their last dinner her husband did that – but it always meant he was close to home.

Meeting Reginald went better than planned. Nigel expected his friend to choose his job – and by extension, his family, and their livelihood – ahead of him.

Nigel looked up and saw he was in front of a house with a pale-yellow door. He raised an eyebrow, and it took him a few breaths to realize he wasn't in front of his house. He was at the door of his neighbors, the Lawlers.

"It's going too far when I pass my own blasted house," Nigel muttered to himself.

He walked up the porch steps of his home and grabbed the handle. Before turning it, though, he turned and looked behind him. Newsboy Cap was out there, and if any connection to Rushforth existed, Nigel was sure he'd see the man again. Satisfied he was alone, and realizing he was being paranoid, Nigel walked inside.

The door creaked. He entered, surprised that no one stood there to greet him. The kitchen was empty. Scratching his head, he walked into the hallway and opened the door to the basement, but it was dark. *They got Charles out of the house? Imagine that.*

Nigel went upstairs, but that was empty as well. "Suppose it's good that Minnie and Ivy have a night out with our dear brother," Nigel said.

He walked back to the kitchen and to the cabinet, pouring himself a brandy. The liquid warmed his gullet on the way down, and after his initial grimace, he savored the oaky flavor.

Between sips, he replayed the events of the last two days in his head. The money-lending house was clearly a front, but for what? Reginald had the mandate from Willoughby to investigate the noble's death, not delve into their alleged shady activities.

"How are the two tied together?" He wondered aloud. Then Nigel realized that, if caught, he'd be concocting scenarios that place doubt and would not only get him fired for good *and* allow Rushforth and his cronies to escape scrutiny.

The door opened to the laughter of two women, and Nigel smiled. He filed away his thoughts on the case for later, set his drink down and walked toward the door.

Charles walked past, his head down and on a beeline for his lab. Nigel continued toward the front door, the laughter louder but the words with it unintelligible.

"Welcome," Nigel said, stopping dead in his tracks at the sight of the man – thinner and standing straighter than Charles ever did - talking to his sister. "Home," he whispered.

The man took off his stovepipe hat and straightened, looking right at Nigel. He was taller – about a forehead higher – with wide shoulders and green eyes that Nigel felt boring into him. His black suit fit him like a glove and was the same color as his handlebar mustache.

"Brother," Minnie said, "You remember Lord Bellamy. We met him at the restaurant, and he was kind enough to walk us home."

Bellamy extended a hand, and Nigel shook it. "Thank you for getting them home safely."

"It is my pleasure, Inspector."

"Care for a cuppa?" Nigel asked.

"That's mighty kind of you, but I should get back. I have an early start tomorrow."

Nigel nodded. Bellamy bowed to Minnie and took his leave.

Ivy came over and squeezed Nigel's arm on the way to the kitchen. Nigel's eyes stayed on Minnie, who tried to force her lips to curve downward, but she couldn't, her smile pasted on her face. She turned away from Nigel.

"You're blushing," Nigel observed.

"Oh dear," Ivy called, returning from the kitchen. "I recall you had a bit more...visceral reaction to me when we were courting."

"You weren't my sister," Nigel said, moving his head toward Ivy, but keeping his eyes on his sister. "And come to think of it, *dear*, there wasn't anything on the social calendar this evening. I know you weren't out engaging in shenanigans, given the current state of affairs."

"Perish the thought," Ivy said, taking a sip of tea.

"Perish the thought indeed," Minnie said.

Nigel looked at them. "What *were* you up to? And how did it catch the eye of an English Lord?"

"Oh you, know," Minnie said. "Being church-bells."

Nigel turned to Ivy. "Like she said, church-bells."

"What kind of Church-bells? Spilling secrets?"

Nigel sat across the kitchen table from Ivy and Minnie, eyes darting back and forth between the two women in his life.

"Darling, I am so very appreciative of your support and willingness to help," Nigel said, then looked to his sister. "And you too, Minnie. But tangling with the aristocracy can lead to trouble. And what's worse, one knows where we live."

"I think you're being irrational," Ivy said.

"Quite irrational," Minnie added.

Nigel sighed, but Ivy leaned forward. "You forget we can take care of ourselves."

"Indeed," Minnie said.

"And besides, no one is going to suspect us two simple ladyfolk for spies."

"What did you find out?"

Ivy turned to Minnie, who sipped her tea. "Not much, unfortunately. We saw a formal gathering going on in West End, but Charles left to admire some new tools he saw in a shop window. By the time I could pry him away, Lord Bellamy showed up."

"Odd that he was there," Nigel said.

"He came from the soiree," Ivy said. "And no, I didn't get an answer what type of party it was. He was enamored with our sister."

Nigel saw Minnie's face redden and she took another sip of tea. "He was a gentleman, through and through, Nigel."

"I wouldn't let him sully our name, my love," Ivy said, smiling at Nigel.

Nigel smiled back. It warmed his heart to know that Ivy thought of them as one unit. Even more reason to understand these mysteries.

"He just asked about me, what I did, our family," Minnie said, shrugging. "The usual."

"So he was just being worthy of his status in life?"

"Nigel," Ivy interjected, "I must prepare you. It felt like beginning a courtship."

Nigel deflated. "Bloody hell."

"Don't be daft, brother," Minnie said, putting the teacup down in the saucer firmer and louder than usual. "I'll be able to improve our station if it works out."

"It's not that, Minnie," Nigel said, just above a whisper. "It's the timing."

"You'll be alright, dear," Ivy said.

Nigel nodded. "Nothing a whiskey and good night's sleep can't fix."

"I'll get that for you."

"Thanks, my love," Nigel said turning to Minnie, who stood.

"I've had quite the night, brother. I'm turning in."

"Good night," Nigel said, sighing as he wondered what else was going to happen before he solved this case.

CHAPTER 19

*W*HUMP. WHUMP. WHUMP.

Nigel's eyes slid open. He was lying on his stomach, right cheek on his pillow. He turned his head to the right.

WHUMP. WHUMP. WHUMP.

Nigel sat up, reached to the edge of the bed and put his pants on. Ivy murmured next to him.

"What is it?" She whispered, in the lull between sleep and being awake.

"Someone's at the door," he replied. "I'll get it."

WHUMP. WHUMP. WHUMP.

Nigel stood and moved to the stairs as fast as his weary legs would take him. "I say!"

He opened the front door just as a bobbie stood there, his hand in the air, ready to knock again.

The police officer still possessed a little roundness to his face, a wide-eyed look as he examined Nigel. *Not used to knocking on doors. Must be his first proper assignment.*

"May I help you?" Nigel asked.

"Beg your pardon for the intrusion so early, sir," The boy said, his voice cracking a bit at the end. "Chief Willoughby would like to see you at the station post haste. He sent a carriage," the bobbie said, gesturing to the hansom behind him. The boy said it in a robotic tone, suggesting he was uttering it from memory, careful not to miss a word.

"I just need a minute to get dressed. Please, come on in."

"Thank you, sir, but my instructions are to wait outside until you join me in the cab."

"Very well," Nigel said. "Just a moment."

Willoughby must want to make some sort of example. Have the neighbors see me go into the cab with a uniformed officer.

If Willoughby was going to take him down, he'd show up himself, with Reginald as a buffer and parade him out, not send a rookie.

So what was the deal?

He grabbed a dress shirt and jacket from the edge of the bed and dressed. Ivy murmured something so quietly, Nigel couldn't understand it.

"Chief wants me at the station," he whispered.

Ivy rubbed her eyes and sat up. "Do you want me to call Father's barrister?"

Nigel shook his head. "Something tells me this isn't a bad thing. Otherwise, Willoughby would be here, making a lot of noise in more than one way."

Nigel walked by Ivy, gently touching her wrist as he passed her. She made a noise that reminded him of a kitten mewing.

"Before you go," Ivy offered. "We should talk about the next steps."

"No time. I'm expected at once," Nigel said, stopping at the base of the stairs. "It's simple. I commiserate with the Chief and go after Rushforth."

"I appreciate your jovial attitude," Ivy said, moving toward him. "But what are we going to do if this doesn't turn out as you expect?"

"I think it works for me either way," Nigel said, taking Ivy's hands in his. "Being an inspector allows me to enter places that a regular person would normally be barred from," Nigel said. "And I can take measures to defend myself."

"If you get caught," Ivy said, pulling her hands back and putting them on her hips. "You risk losing almost everything."

She moved forward, wrapping her arms around Nigel's waist. Immediately, he felt her warmth move throughout his body, and he closed his eyes, trying to preserve the moment.

"I cannot bear the thought of being apart from you," Nigel said, putting his arms around Ivy. "But I cannot shake the thought of the families of those poor women, having to send their loved ones to God without knowing why they are gone."

Nigel pulled back to look her in the eyes. He dared not look too long, for he knew he could get lost in them. "And while I've come to learn that you are more than capable of defending yourself, I cannot continue this life if you are not here on Earth with me. I will not chance you, or my dear sister, being a victim. Not while I can do something about it."

She smiled at him. "I love you for all of that, my darling, and I cannot fathom a future without you."

Nigel smiled at her.

"We still have to be smart," Ivy said.

Nigel kissed her finger, then pulled her hand into his. "That's why I have to get moving on solving this case."

Ivy gestured for him to come to her, and she took his face in her hands and kissed him. "For luck."

He smiled and went downstairs. The young cop, who was now waiting by the cab, opened the door for him. Nigel got in. The bobbie sat across from him, banging his head on the roof as he sat opposite Nigel. The cab started moving.

"Did the chief say what he needed me for?" Nigel asked. The bobbie shook his head and looked away.

So it's going to be a quiet ride, then.

***

The cab reached the station, and the bobbie jumped up and opened the door first. He did it so swiftly that if he wasn't holding on to the door, he would have fallen right out.

Nigel chuckled as quiet as possible while he watched this, but assumed a neutral expression as he got out. He started for the entrance, but the rookie snapped his fingers. Nigel whipped his head around to look at him, raising an eyebrow.

"Forgive me sir, but the chief would like you to go in through the back."

Well, Nigel thought to himself, *this is on the hush and hush. Now I'm really confused as to what's going on.*

Nigel nodded and walked in through the back entrance, right to Willoughby's office. The door was ajar, and Nigel heard two men conversing, but couldn't make out what they were saying. With a knock, he entered the room.

Intending to defy the chief, Nigel's gaze landed on the man seated across from him: Lord Bellamy, who seemed to be clad in an outfit identical to the previous night, except it was a dark blue instead of black. He maintained the same friendly expression but betrayed nothing else.

"Nigel, thanks for coming," Willoughby said. "Lord Bellamy wished to speak to you, but decorum necessitated he do it away from your home. He suggested that, since you were in my department, he could do it here."

And since you worship at the feet of noblemen, Nigel thought, *you'd do just what he wanted, Chief.*

Nigel nodded.

"My humblest apologies for waking you this early," Bellamy said. "I have a business meeting this morning and had to pass by the station. I knew you weren't here but did not realize this was your day off."

Nigel looked at Willoughby and nodded for that small kindness. "It's no problem at all, my lord."

"I wish to gain your permission to call on your sister. She is a fine woman, and I look forward to getting to know her. With your blessing, of course."

Of all the things that I thought this meeting would entail, this request was not it.

Bellamy betrayed no emotion as he looked at Nigel. Clearly, this was not something he was accustomed to or had experienced before, so he just sat there.

Nigel felt the power wash over him. For a slight moment, he held the fate of a Noble in his hand. *If only my investigation can go this way,* he thought to himself.

Still, Minnie lit up when she talked about Bellamy, not to mention what this will mean for their whole family, Charles included. Nigel felt he only had one direction he could go.

"You have my blessing. Thank you for asking."

Bellamy nodded instead, once again offering his hand and Nigel, who took it. "I look forward to getting to know your family better."

"Likewise, my Lord."

"Thank you for coming in, Nigel," Willoughby said. " I certainly don't want to take up any more of your time or your day off."

In other words, Nigel thought to himself, *get out of here.*

He nodded, tipped his cap, and walked out.

***

Ivy and Minnie both beamed tapping their feet nervously as Nigel shared the news.

"Thank you," Minnie said.

"Just don't cock it up," he said with a wink. Ivy stuck her tongue out in mock indignation, then turned to Minnie who reached out and adjusted the collar of her dress.

A knock on the door stopped them in their tracks. Nigel went to get it, his sister right behind him. He turned to her putting his hand up as if to tell her to relax. She took a deep breath.

Nigel answered the door and Lord Bellamy stood there.

"Forgive me for showing up earlier than agreed," Bellamy said. "My meeting ended early, and well, I was in the neighborhood."

"Come on in my lord," Nigel said.

Bellamy nodded. Nigel stepped aside so Minnie could greet him. They smiled at each other, and Minnie gestured for them to go to the front sitting room. Ivy waited about five heartbeats before coming in with tea. Nigel walked to the stairs, stopping at the bottom to turn and look at his sister and her new suitor. They were whispering and laughing. It reminded Nigel of his courtship with Ivy.

His wife stepped in his sightline, no doubt to signify that he should give his sister some privacy, but her smile suggested she was thinking the same thing. "I'm going to go work on the case," he said.

Ivy nodded and returned to the kitchen.

If there's any justice in the universe, I will not have any daughters. This is driving me crazy now, this courting of my sister by nobility. I can't imagine how crazy is going to be with my own children.

But if he didn't solve this case soon, any future children will be the least of his worries. Nigel walked upstairs as fast as he could and cracked open his files, getting to work.

— • —

CHAPTER 20

Beulah Kerrigan opened her eyes, but the darkness remained. She blinked a few times to make sure they were open. To her right, a flicker entered her peripheral vision. Candles were lit about an arm's length from her shoulder. She looked to her left, and candles were aflame, but only lit the surrounding area. Beulah couldn't recall where she was.

She remembered a man of impeccable dress, his suit crisp and sharp as his eyes, which mimicked her blue ones. Yes, her suitor, the noble! Who had graciously provided a covered seat in the rear of his carriage for her cousin, serving as chaperone. Beulah remembered his charming smile, and his earnest interest in her likes and dreams. He differed from other men who inquired about her hand. It seemed too good to be true.

What happened that I'm here? She recalled getting into the carriage and accepting a tiny glass of wine as they made their way to dinner. *Oh my, am I home? Did I drink too much?* The blood rushed to her head. This was awful. If she drank too much, her cousin, Agatha, would end the affair and inform her father, and that would be the end of courting this season.

Strands of her strawberry blonde hair fell into her eyes. Beulah lifted her hand, but it only moved a few inches. She tried again, same result.

Her hands were strapped down to a large slab of concrete. Her breath came quick, and she closed her eyes, inhaling long to calm herself.

"Hello? Is anyone here?"

Beulah waited, but no one answered. She asked again. Nothing. She opened her mouth to ask louder, but the sound of deep chanting gave her pause. To her it sounded like the opening procession of church, the only thing missing was the smell of burning incense.

The chanting grew louder, mixed in with regimented footfalls on the floor. She lifted her head to see six men enter, clad in dark purple robes. On the front, a half moon connected to a type of Christian cross, one Beulah had never seen before: there was a second horizontal bar below the first.

The men formed a circle around the stone slab she laid on. "Where are we? Let me go!"

They didn't answer, instead continuing their chant.

"Please, what is going on? Help me!"

The chanting stopped, and one man moved to the base of the slab. Even in the loose robe, she could tell he was muscular, his arms and torso almost filling the robes out. The man looked upward, started speaking in a language Beulah wasn't familiar with. At the end of each stanza, his voice raised, and the rest of the men chanted.

"Please, why won't you help me? Please!"

The man chanted in a low voice as he crawled onto the slab over Beulah. She struggled, but someone had tied her hands and feet. She screamed as he cut her gown.

He spoke in a low voice as he put the knife against her bosom. Her voice, almost gone from repeated pleas, screamed as the man put a slit between her breasts, then another on her right abdomen and her left side.

In a few heartbeats, it was a chore to breathe. The last thing she remembered was the man, crowding around her, slurping her blood.

CHAPTER 21

Nigel scratched his head, leaning back in his chair. He closed his eyes, rifling through the cabinets and shelves of his memory. With access to the bulk of case files now being impossible, he had to recall a lot from memory. Fortunately, recent events were still fresh in his mind. Mallory Finance, Newsboy Cap, and the murder of the girls. The slits in their body and the location and the fact that they were wearing white gowns all made it into the newspapers. But cases were won with minor details, and attention to them, and Nigel figured he needed to solve this more than ever.

Nigel rubbed his right hand, cramping from the flurry of writing. He hadn't done this much with a pen and paper since grammar school. He took a deep breath and looked at it when he wrote it down. Nothing else came to mind, so he got up and paced back and forth. Nigel stretched, took in the sight of the city outside his window. Nothing. Feeling that a distraction could help. *Seeing Charles in his lab is just the ticket.*

Charles was at his woodworking station, a welding torch in hand. His goggles only just covered his eyes, a fact that made Nigel laugh. Despite his brother's mental condition, he was a smart man regarding safety. Nigel was not happy with his choice of eye protection, and made it known. Charles insisted that there was no risk of his eyes being injured, and further attempts to argue did nothing, so he stopped.

Nigel stepped back, a respectful distance away from his brother, waiting for him to finish. His brother attempted to weld two pieces of brass together, but it wasn't clear what he was trying to make. Someone not familiar with his brother's methods wouldn't blame them for thinking it was the beginnings of a telescope. Charles intimated, in his way, that this was the first step in something much larger, which wouldn't be clear until he was done.

Charles put down his tools, removing his goggles to look at what he made. He saw Nigel and faced him.

"Brother, I need your help with something," Nigel said. "I need to take notes, but unfortunately my brain moves faster than my hands. I'm sure you understand this issue.

"Do you have something that can record my voice, and save whatever I speak, so I can take notes later?"

Charles shook his head.

"Something told me that would be the case. Not even you have made everything you have in that mind of yours. Just so you know brother, my birthday is coming up."

He eyed the item on Charles's desk. "What are you making there?"

"Tinker toy," Charles said.

Nigel laughed. "Wonders never cease. Charles, do you remember my friend Reginald? He may stop by. If he needs something that you have, that you're not using, will you let him borrow it? I can vouch for him."

"Good man," Charles said. Nigel knew he would have no problem sharing his work with Reginald. He patted his brother on the shoulder and walked upstairs, hearing some laughter.

Minnie and Ivy were in the kitchen, making some tea. Nigel smiled. "How'd it go?"

"Tell you when it's over," Ivy whispered.

"Maybe," Minnie added, grabbing the tray and walking to the sitting room. Nigel shook his head. A *tick-tick, tick, tick-tick* sound filled his eardrums.

He walked to the telegraph, and sure enough, it spit out a message. Nigel's heart thumped harder and faster for a moment. *This can't be good.*

Nigel picked the tape up and read it. *Got information on the policemen's benefit. Asked to be seated near you. Informed you're not attending. Is there a reason for me to worry? L*

It was one thing to have nosy in-laws; that went with marriage. *But with the suspension and their previous heated interactions, Lovelace had concerns, and he voiced them. The timing wasn't good. Has it ever been with him, since you wed Ivy? I look forward to moments when Lovelace and I can discuss things over brandy as father-in-law and son.*

Nigel put the tape down. *Time to deal with this once Bellamy leaves.* He wasn't as flat-footed as some bobbies, but Nigel took deliberate steps to minimize noise. He stood by the kitchen door, but other than an occasional chuckle, he couldn't make out anything.

Nigel bemoaned him not having any brandy right now, as he thought of a way to explain things to Lovelace. Would he go with the trope of 'I was fired, but not really fired'? Where Willoughby has him deep undercover and would deny anything? That seemed to be the most logical choice.

Nigel exhaled, pacing. That would work in the short term but would show Lovelace that his son-in-law is not above deceit. Plus, Lovelace would want him to have a plan on how Nigel would provide a good life for Ivy with a new job.

He tossed that thought from his mind and turned to his sister instead. What did that mean for Minnie? Sure, Lord Bellamy is courting her, but that doesn't mean that it will go far. A man of his stature had options. He felt content with Ivy being involved as her chaperone, and he didn't want to impose on her, but having her on the marriage path now would be ideal.

You won't help matters if you're caught snooping. Nigel returned to his desk, letting the case flood his mind. Like before, he let bits and pieces come first, some leading to longer paths, like the first Jane Doe case. Every detail flowed from his brain to his fingers holding the stylus. He remembered the cuts in detail, the hair as bright as sunflowers, and the bloody gown.

Nigel continued building the cases, oblivious to the world around him. To his sister's laugh, to the *clink* of the teacups in saucers, to the looming shadow on the wall getting bigger. He didn't hear the odd footfall creaking the wooden floor, nor feel the room temperature rise, and the hot breath of the person coming up behind him.

Nigel was so engrossed, he didn't realize there was a hand on his shoulder until the hand squeezed. As a reflex, Nigel took the stylus and gripped it as he would a knife, holding it over the hand.

"Bread," Charles said behind him.

Nigel relaxed his grip on the stylus and set it down. "Charles, you can't sneak up on people like that."

"No answer."

"Really? Then my heartfelt apologies, brother. Been a rough couple of days. My mind is elsewhere."

"Not good, always looking away."

"I know, Charles. Anyway, what do you need?"

"Bread. Need fuel."

"Got it. Should have a new loaf here," Nigel said, walking over to the cabinet about the bread drawer. He pulled out a loaf and handed it to his brother. who nodded and took it back to the lab. Nigel smiled. *Some days I wish life was simpler. Charles, despite his challenges, is at peace with himself. And he has a passion that will change lives. I'm just a copper.*

Nigel tried to recapture his focus and output, but the break with Charles halted his momentum. He sat there, eyes closed, retracing steps. Some of it came back, and he jotted additional details down. He thought Ivy came in to say Bellamy left and wished him good night, but it might have been Minnie.

Nigel shook his head and rubbed his eyes; staring at the parchment thing long made his vision blurry. He figured it'd be a good time to let it rest. Grabbing his notebook, Nigel went through his list of contacts, making a note next to people he wanted to talk to and those who'd be open to speaking because of their friendly connection, not the badge.

The floor creaked with heavier footsteps, and this time, Nigel heard them. He smiled.

"Back for seconds?" He said, turning around.

Instead of his brother, he saw the cold metal of a knife inches from his heart.

***

Nigel grabbed Lord Bellamy's wrist, keeping the knife from plunging into his chest. He grimaced; the man was stronger than he looked.

"This won't...do favors...for you in our wedding...negotiations," Nigel said. Bellamy smiled an eerie grin. He carried more weight, and used it, leaning into Nigel, who had to step back. His knees were straining, his wrists screaming in pain, threatening to rip.

This wasn't a battle Nigel was going to win, so he didn't fight. He loosened himself and retreated a step. Bellamy fell forward, and Nigel leapt onto his back, knocking him to the ground. The aristocrat cried out and rolled over, trying to crush Nigel, but he kneed the noble in his hip.

In order to avoid harm, Bellamy groaned and moved, allowing Nigel to roll out of the way. The noble got to his knees faster than Nigel expected, swinging the knife wildly. Nigel feigned a full-on attack, and Bellamy took the bait, overextending enough to allow the inspector to grab his wrist.

Nigel pulled with all his might, but Bellamy held his grip firm. The noble elbowed his opponent in the chin and swung the knife. It sliced his arm in the area between the shoulder and bicep. He groaned. Bellamy punched it, pain shooting throughout Nigel's arm. He hit the ground, and the knife missed his head by half a yard.

But that didn't matter. As Nigel backed up, Bellamy moved over him.

He let Bellamy take a step forward and kicked him in the knee. He fell, and Nigel sat up.

Both men stopped when a scream rang out behind them. Minnie charged toward them, anger in her eyes.

Bellamy got up and Minnie ran to him, feigning an attack on his knees, then kicking the aristocrat in the chest. He stumbled back toward Nigel who pushed him back. Bellamy turned and put his fists up.

Neither of them saw Ivy come in with a rolling pin, swinging it in Bellamy's face. Minnie kicked him in the groin after he stumbled back into her. He doubled over and Ivy rushed in, smacking him in the back with the rolling pin. Bellamy fell to his knees.

Nigel couldn't move.

Bellamy recovered, reaching for Ivy's leg and she aimed a kick toward his face. He caught her leg and pulled it. She fell to the ground.

Ivy cried out and her eyes met Nigel's.

Rage rose in him, his face warm as the blood rose there. He clenched his fist and slid toward the knife that laid on the ground.

Bellamy reached for it as well, but Minnie saw this and jumped onto Bellamy's back and they fell onto the floor. Nigel lunged forward and grabbed the knife. Bellamy tried to get up and attack, but Nigel plunged the knife into his stomach. The noble didn't go down right away, so Nigel twisted the knife. Bellamy grimaced, a guttural sound caught in his throat. His eyes, once widened, now fluttering became shallow, then stopped. Nigel leaned over him and felt nothing escape Bellamy's mouth. The nobleman was dead.

Minnie rushed over to Nigel, collapsing by his side, her breath short and frantic.

"Are you okay?" Minnie asked.

Nigel looked at the cut on him. "I'll live," he said, looking at Ivy, and slid toward her.

"Darling?" Nigel said.

"I'm all right," Ivy said.

"You got stabbed," Minnie said.

"He just cut me a little."

"I'll be the judge of that, love," Ivy said.

"Why was Bellamy attacking you?"

"I'm not sure," Nigel said, relaying to the women how Bellamy came upon him. "But that is not the important matter to discuss. Where did you two learn to fight?"

Ivy looked at Minnie, who nodded. "Husband, it's about time you know something."

"Which is?"

"We are your Bird Demons."

CHAPTER 22

Nigel's mouth stayed agape and he asked, "I beg your pardon?"

"I saw your notes the other day," Minnie said. "That some called us Bird Demons. We thought it was cute. My friends call us the Petticoat Society."

"I quite like that one," Ivy said.

"Ladies, please," Nigel said. "I think the blood loss is affecting me because I am hallucinating."

"You're not, darling," Ivy said, sitting down next to him. "Minnie, please go get me something to clean this, will you?"

"But what about-"

"I want to make sure Nigel doesn't bleed out."

Minnie left the room.

"It is just a cut, you know," Ivy said. "But we shouldn't let it get worse."

"I'm not worried about the bloody cut," Nigel growled. "What the hell do you mean you're the Bird Demons?"

"Started as a conversation, really," Minnie said, re-entering with bandages and alcohol, which she gave to Ivy. "During launch, Katherine Willard told us about a suitor who tried to take advantage of her. She got away, thank the Lord-"

"Thank the Lord," Ivy said.

"But she wished she had a leather petticoat, it might have been easier to fight him off, if he couldn't get in," Minnie continued. "And she said her brother was stabbed, but because he wore a leather blacksmith vest, it was only a flesh wound."

"We took that to heart and ordered them," Ivy said. "It was a great idea for your sister, as she was about to make her debut."

"Then Mary Kane was killed," Minnie said, looking at Nigel. "The first girl murdered. She was one of my best friends as a child before her father got a new job. We wrote letters and kept in touch.

"There are girls in my situation dying. I would not be a victim."

"I would not let her become one, either," Ivy added. "She is my sister, and I was once in her shoes."

"And the dresses?" Nigel asked.

"Last year, we went shopping as we prepped for the wedding," Minnie told him. "We purchased pink dresses. It was such a good deal, we got tailoring with it."

"One of the wonderful things with that deal," Ivy said, "Is we made it double sided. It was black on the inside because of the fabric, so we just had him make us an extra dress."

"So we wear black when we-"

"Wait a minute," Nigel said, wincing. "*You killed a nobleman?*"

"Yes."

"So that was your bits of pink fabric I found near the scenes. Bloody hell," Nigel said, collapsing on the ground. Ivy grabbed his arm.

"Darling, are you okay?"

"NO! My wife and sister are killers, and I am a police inspector."

"I thought the Chief demoted you?" Minnie asked.

Nigel stared daggers at her. "Do you know the position this puts me in?" His eyes bored into Ivy. "Here *and* at work?"

"We've been careful," Minnie said.

"And it's just the nobles who killed the women."

Nigel perked up at that. "What? Do you have proof of that?"

"Well, no," Ivy said. "But they were the men that the women were going to see when they died."

"How do you know that?"

"My friends and I talked over tea," Minnie said.

"I wish you would have come to me with this earlier," Nigel said, eyeing both of them. "We could have done something serious about it. As such, they know I'm getting close. My wife and sister murdered two men and I've got powerful people who want me removed from my position, if not killed."

He tried to stand, and both Ivy and Minnie helped him. "Thank you. I am convinced that tonight's attack is Rushforth's doing."

"How so?" Ivy asked.

"The finance office for one. And it seemed a little too convenient that he knew about Charles."

"Maybe it was Bellamy?" Minnie offered.

"Even the simplest person could tell Bellamy was earnest in wanting to court you," Nigel said. "I found his discovery of our brother's work to be farfetched."

"So why do you think he attacked?"

"I believe Rushforth sent him to finish what needed to be done," Nigel speculated.

Minnie's foot falls on the stairs echoed throughout the house, so Nigel stopped talking.

"I'll talk with her later," Ivy said.

Minnie handed Ivy bandages and a bowl of water, and Nigel's wife finished cleaning the wound.

Minnie sat down, eyeing Bellamy's corpse. "A part of me figured he was too good to be true."

"We have to get rid of the body."

"Of course, dear. No one will think of looking in the basement."

"I cannot believe you just suggested that, Ivy," Nigel said. "The Petticoats are done."

"I meant you should call on Reginald."

"I thought of calling him myself."

"Questions will be asked," Minnie said, "And given recent events, might not look good."

"Minnie, you've known Reginald most of your life, and he's been my friend just as long. I trust him, and for us to get through this, we will need his assistance."

"I hate it when you're right," Minnie grumbled.

"Once Reginald is here, it might be best for the two of you to just disappear. And maybe take certain outfits with you."

"We can go to my parents' house under the ruse of having to recover from the trauma," Ivy said, tying the bandage on Nigel's arm. "You cooperate with the police to clear yourself of any wrongdoing."

"Excellent. Now, let's see how fast your father's telegram device will work."

***

Reginald came by in one of his "about town" suits that always made Nigel laugh. one to wear black, gray or dark blue, Reginald's attire often had bright green, dark orange or red. His wife bought them as a gift for their nights out. Reginald hated them. He wore dark red tonight, fitting for the situation at hand.

"Thank you for your discretion, old friend."

"You're lucky I stepped out of the house in this."

"Let me show you why," Nigel said, walking to the kitchen.

Nigel stepped aside and looked down at Bellamy's corpse. Reginald looked at the body, then at his friend.

"This is a right awful mess, isn't it?" he moved closer, crouching down next to the body. "Is that Lord Bellamy?"

"That it is."

"Didn't he want to work with Charles and court Minnie?"

Nigel recounted the story for him, and Reginald took it all in, eyes never leaving the corpse.

"The girls left already?"

"Yes, with an appropriate cover story."

"Good. This is going to be tricky enough as it is, without getting anyone else involved. What about your brother?"

"In the lab, asleep. He saw nothing."

"Any copper worth his station, not to mention a lawyer would question him, since Bellamy reached out to him. They'll finagle whatever they can, and you know it."

"Should I get us counsel?"

"It'd cast doubt on you, and that's the last thing you need. Give me some time, and I'll figure something out. We'll get the body out tonight. Just be careful. Trouble seems to have a nasty habit of following you around. Do your best to shake it."

CHAPTER 23

Nigel stirred, eyes darting open, breathing labored. He was in bed in his home. Smelling lavender assaulted his nostrils. He turned towards it, but Ivy was gone. As he wiped the sleep from his eyes, he remembered she took Minnie to his in-laws.

It was only one night, but he admitted to himself that he missed her. Despite everything that happened, Ivy was at his side, a true partner. There weren't many situations he couldn't handle - the death of his parents when he was young saw to that - but it was nice to know Ivy was there for him.

Then he recalled the events of the previous evening, and the woman he loved had killed –justified or not – and that scared him a little.

Not because he feared she'd turn on him, but that it might be discovered and he'd lose her forever.

Nigel went downstairs. Charles walked by him, bread in hand, on the way to his lab. He checked the teapot – it was filled - and turned the stove on.

While the pot heated, Nigel's thoughts turned to Lovelace. There was no sense in delaying a meeting, but he wanted to go into it with a plan.

He took a breath in, and something wrinkled his nose, like wafts of rotting eggs and fish.

"Blimey," Nigel said. "Didn't get all the smell."

He went into the closet and pulled out a broom, bucket and brush. The teapot went off and he poured himself a cup. Making sure the pot was empty, he took out the tea leaves and put them on the floor. He swept them up and got tallet and olive oil from the pantry and mixed them in the bucket. He pulled up his sleeves and crouched down to scrub the spot with the strongest smell.

The tedium and repetitive motion of the work engrossed Nigel and allowed him to forget the events of the previous evening, if only long enough to get the smell out.

"I'm surprised you're awake," Minnie said as she walked into the kitchen, putting her overnight bag down.

"One could say the same about you. Don't debutantes sleep until noon?"

"Let's see how *you* fare when your deranged, would-be suitor lies dead on your kitchen floor."

"Touché, sister. Where is Ivy?"

"She went right up to bed. Didn't sleep well. The small office her father made from her old room had a couch as hard as your head, apparently. She didn't sleep a wink."

"I should think not, especially given her actions," Nigel stood and put the brush in the bucket, looking at Minnie. "*Both* of your actions."

"Troubled?"Minnie offered in reply.

Nigel nodded. "I am vexed, least of all by this Petticoat Society business. As for the girls, I'm missing something."

"You've always been good at solving puzzles, dear brother. One of my earliest memories is sitting up watching you work on a puzzle of Big Ben."

"Is that so?" Nigel asked, smiling at that revelation. "You're right, but that was a toy. Now they involve death and maniacs. But it's what I know, and the one thing I'm good at."

Minnie laughed. Nigel poured them both a cup of tea.

"You're an adequate big brother.

"Such loving sentiments."

Minnie smiled. "What now?"

"I hoped that with time and Earl Grey, I'd arrive at a solution."

"Well-"

Loud banging on the door cut Minnie's words off.

"It's not enough that I've had quite the evening, now one must induce ringing in my head?" Nigel said.

He strode to the front door, flinging it open. "Alright, already!"

He froze upon seeing Reginald standing there, his expression somber.

"You look like someone died."

Reginald stepped aside to allow Willoughby to step forward. He was upright, meaty hands behind his back. And if Nigel didn't know better, his lips twitched toward a smile.

"Nigel Barrington, you are under arrest for the murder of Lord Bellamy. You *do* not *have* to say anything. But it may harm your defense if you *do* not mention when questioned something which you later rely on in court. Anything you *do* or say may be given in evidence."

"Chief, this is all wrong. Did you get the report?"

"Nigel," Reginald said, shaking his head.

Willoughby turned to Nigel, holding brass handcuffs. "If you please."

Reginald paused, taking a step back from his boss. Willoughby's eyebrows dropped, his gaze intense. He shook the cuffs once.

"Do what you must," Nigel said.

Reginald sighed, taking the cuffs. "Please turn around."

Nigel complied, and Reginald fit the cuffs on.

"I didn't know what the chief needed me for until we got here. Otherwise, I would've declined."

"I had an inkling this would happen," Nigel whispered. "Just do me a favor."

"Anything."

"Keep an eye on my family."

"Consider it done," Reginald said.

He turned Nigel around to face the Chief Inspector, who sneered, "After you, *murderer*."

Nigel walked to the police carriage, ignoring the gathered neighbors and onlookers. Reginald sat next to him, Willoughby taking up most of the seat across from him, a smug smile on his face. Nigel turned his head, not giving his former boss the satisfaction.

He also didn't want to do or say something to make the situation worse. That didn't prevent him from making quick mental calculations of where to strike Willoughby for maximum pain entered his mind. His muscles tightened, his breathing heavy and quick.

As the carriage pulled away, Nigel saw Ivy and Minnie in the doorway with Reginald by their side. They stood with their shoulders up, but their eyes betrayed their fear and sadness.

Nigel exhaled and looked down. In his attempt to take care of his wife and siblings, he ultimately failed. He leaned his head against the wall, the shadows covering most of his face.

Feeling light-headed, he looked over at Willoughby, whose head appeared to be moving in a circular motion. Nigel shut his eyes tight, counted to three in his head and opened them. Willoughby was once again still.

His stomach twirled, and Nigel had to concentrate on his breathing for the sensation to dissipate. He let his family down and they were not safe. But that would have to wait until he could get out of this mess he was in.

As the carriage made another turn, Nigel swore he could see Lord Rushforth, across the street, a toothy grin on his face.

***

The Tower of London still held prisoners in the 19th century. Many were of the political variety, or dangers to the Queen or Royal Family, but they were there, hidden in the basement levels.

Nigel knew of this, as did his fellow inspectors. They thought it was rumor at first, but the Jack the Ripper investigation brought it to the fore, as people thought that the murderer, if not killed, would spend the rest of his days in the Tower.

As the carriage pulled up, the Tower taking up the whole of his view, Nigel wasn't sure if he should be flattered or scared.

Then Rushforth's smiling visage popped into his head. *He's the reason I'm here, no doubt.*

The carriage stopped. Willoughby got out, gesturing for Reginald to remove Nigel. In a small show of defiance, which Nigel appreciated, Reginald only guided his friend out of the carriage.Willoughby stood next to him.

"Let's go, Barrington. You're moving into your new, permanent residence."

"Sir, I'd like to see this through," Reginald said.

"Very well, but you will follow us, and only speak when spoken to."

"Thank you, sir."

Willoughby tugged at Nigel's arm, leading him toward the side of the tower and onto a beach that got narrower as they went.

We're going to St. John's Tower.

From there, they hopped in a boat and rowed to a metal gate that opened on two sides, with lattice work above them, also made of metal. This was the infamous Traitor's Gate, where the Tudors sent members of the Royal family accused of plotting against them.

At the gate, two members of Yeomen Warders of Her Majesty's Royal Palace and Fortress the Tower of London, or Beefeaters, their colloquial title amongst commoners, stood.

The Chief Inspector made it a point to inform the guard that Nigel was his former employee and that his misdeeds were the only black mark on his precinct. The guard opened the gate, and Willoughby led Nigel inside, where the Chief Warden came out to meet him.

Like many of the wardens, he was an older man. He had graying hair, the sideburns the most prominent. He clasped Willoughby's wrist. A quiet exchange between them elicited laughter that echoed in the halls before the Chief Warden turned to Nigel.

"What kind of special scum made you leave the comforts of your posh office to grace me with your presence?"

"A rotten one," Willoughby said, recounting the death of Lord Bellamy.

"A special kind, indeed. No worries, Chief Inspector, we'll take good care of him from here."

"Of that, I'm sure."

Willoughby left, and the Beefeaters slammed the gate shut, the echo of the metal ringing in Nigel's ears. One guard, on the Chief Warden's gesture, grabbed Nigel's arm and led him deeper into the bowels of the Tower.

The warden, whom Nigel discovered was named Carlisle, opened every gate with a master set of keys, which comprised one key with three different heads that could be removed or snapped into place. Nigel filed that away for future reference.

"Get a move on, you swine."

"Swine? I was brought into the traitor's gate entrance. That's only reserved for royalty."

"Think you're clever, do ya? The only royal thing you'll get in here is a whuppin'!"

He took Nigel's arm and led him into the prison level of the Tower. A few of the cells were akin to boarding rooms for single migrant workers. They had a bed, table, books. The corner one even had a servant outside, nice suit and white gloves, ready to provide whatever the prisoner needed. *Wonder if it's for a member of the royal family to get this treatment.*

The cells were less grandiose and more rank the further they went, and it was in one of these cells that Carlisle deposited Nigel.

"Enjoy your new home, rat!" Carlisle said, chuckling as he went away. Nigel smiled and waved, which erased the grin from the head Beefeater's face. When he was gone, Nigel turned and took in his surroundings.

The sheets on the bed looked like they were purloined from a home about to be torn down. The frame itself was sunken inward. There was a wooden chair that didn't look big enough for a young child, let alone a grown man. And the chamber pot looked to be a relic of the days of Richard the Lionheart.

It wasn't empty, either.

"Right then," Nigel said, taking a seat on the edge of the bed that looked just capable of holding his weight.

Nigel saw the sun's reflection make its way from the bottom of his cell toward the top, and guessed it was about midday. His rumbling stomach confirmed his suspicion. He didn't expect the Warden to send him food. The stories he heard of the place suggested it would be as uncomfortable as possible for him,especially as a former public servant.

He hoped Ivy would use her father's connections to get some legal remedy prepared, though Nigel didn't hold his breath, as Ivy would likely be required to reveal more than either of them wanted. Still, he had rights, and they'd be seen to sooner rather than later. *That* he counted on, because if they were going to convict, the Crown would be sure to show everyone they played straight.

There was nothing to do but wait, Nigel thought. *So that's what I'll do.*

***

The Order of the Patriarchal Crescent gathered in the rotunda of their sacred temple, dressed in the black ceremonial robes of the order. The symbol of the group, a crescent moon against a Patriarchal Cross, was over each of their hearts, a reminder that the order was part of their blood.

Candles lit on pillars around the circle provided illumination enough to see where one was going, but not much else. They stood in a circle, enclosed save for the top,where the Supreme Master would stand. Echoes of footsteps against marble filled the chamber, and the gathered members bowed as their leader took his place, closing the circle.

The Master lifted his head, allowing a glimpse of his bearded chin. "The impediment has been removed. It is time to call forth the Illuminated."

"But what of the reports?" an older voice wheezed to the master's right. "They have not quieted, and our brothers face significant risk."

"Now that there are no more obstacles, we can work to protect our organization."

A deeper, robust voice to the master's left said, "We require another offering to ensure favor."

"The selection has been made. We just need to procure it."

***

The knot in Reginald's tie still would not form correctly, so he took it off, throwing it on the ground in disgust. In the mirror, his wife stood in the doorway, hands on her hips.

"I just bought that for you Christmas. I can't believe you're sick of it already."

"It's not that."

"I'm just teasing, husband," She looked up at his face. "What's the matter?"

He relayed the trip to the Tower of London with Nigel. His beloved tightened up and dropped to a chair with equal measure,and she covered her mouth with her hand, gasping.

"I, I can't believe it. We've known Nigel for years, he would never do something like that."

"He wouldn't. Something's afoot." He relayed to her the case they were working on, in generalities. Reginald was never, on his best day, the detective that Nigel was. He knew they would break through soon with the actions of yesterday.Someone was impeding progress.

"So what are you going to do?"

"If I ever get this tie to work, my job and figure out how I can save my friend."

His wife took his hand sat him on the bed and put her hand on his knee and smiled. "You're a wonderful husband and father, Reginald. And a good cop. I know you'll solve this."

She picked the tie up, creating a perfect knot. Reginald grabbed her in his arms, squeezing her tight. *This is going to be the roughest day of my life. At least I have her by my side.*

***

Reginald practiced his speech on the way to the precinct. With Nigel in jail, Willoughby asked him to take charge of the noble killing investigation. He had plenty of reasons to decline, starting with his friendship to Nigel - which would not win him many points with the boss —to illness or his lack of skill as a detective. None of them would pass muster, he mused.

Ironically, as he walked under the light by the front door of the precinct, an idea hit him. Yes, Reginald was not like his friend. And while he would appear to stay neutral on the matter of Nigel's guilt or innocence, being so close to the case would hamper the investigation. Given the priority Willoughby and nobles like Rushforth placed on the case, that was not something that they could afford.

Satisfied with the decision, he tried to make his way to his desk, but there were simply too many people in the way. Mike, the young bobbie, directed people. Reginald walked up and tapped him on the shoulder.

"What is going on, my good man?"

"It's a nightmare, sir. Willoughby wants to see you in his office straight away."

Reginald nodded, weaving his way through the gathered throng. After what seemed like hours, he finally shoved his way through the crowd and into his boss's office.

"You wished to see me, sir?"

Willoughby turned, and Reginald saw his face was red. "Ah, Reginald, we have a crisis."

"Another murder?"

"No, something from the Devil Himself. Those damn bird demons are real."

Reginald blink. "Beg your pardon, sir?"

"Multiple sightings are pouring in of two birds, clad in black and pink dresses, stalked the streets of Whitechapel last night. A couple of men saw them as the sun rose, and they disappeared. People are worried."

"Are we going to entertain such notions?"

"I thought it was all poppycock, and I used it to teach Nigel a lesson and get him back to the basics of police work. As you can see, the number of claims warrant investigation."

"I'll be happy to take the lead on this, sir." *Especially since I don't want to step on Nigel's toes and do anything that would hamper his case.*

"Good man Reginald. I knew I could count on you. Go see Michael at the front desk, and he will give you the details."

Reginald saluted and got out of the office as fast as he could, hoping Willoughby would not change his mind.

Outside, he looked over notes that the young officer Michael had taken. Four witnesses saw the demons confined to a certain area, on the fringes of Whitechapel, near the homes of prominent Lords. And they were close to a certain house he frequented. Reginald figured it would be a good place to start.

***

Ivy answered the door in a simple house dress, smile as wide the city of London, welcoming him inside.

"This is an unexpected pleasure, Reginald. Though the timing is less than ideal."

"How are you holding up?"

"My husband is in jail for murder and all I can do is beg Charles and Minnie to help keep me from losing all of my nerves."

"I cannot imagine what you are going through."

"No, you cannot. Cuppa? It's Earl Gray," Ivy said.

"Thank you," Reginald nodded, and Ivy poured him a cup.

"Are you here with an update on Nigel?"

"As much as I wish that were the case, I have some questions to ask you."

Ivy's face remained neutral.

"There's no easy way to do this," Reginald said with a sigh, "So I'm just going to come out and say it. Where were you last night around 10 p.m.?"

"I beg your pardon?"

"I know it sounds unorthodox, but the sooner you answer, the quicker I can leave."

Ivy took a sip of her tea, her eyes never leaving Reginald's. "Either in bed or preparing to be. May I ask what this is about?"

Reginald informed her of the various sightings from the hundreds of people inside the precinct. Ivy did her best to stifle a laugh. "I've heard some quite fanciful notions in my day, but that's an original one."

Reginald studied her for a minute, exhaling as he answered. "Me too. With everything going on with your husband, I figured I'd head here first and rule you out right away. Things will not be easy for him, and we must give him every advantage. If you should have come across anything resembling what we discussed today, please call me right away. It is of the utmost importance."

"I will," Ivy said touching Reginald hand.

"If you need anything, please don't hesitate."

"Thank you, and for Nigel's sake, good luck."

— • —

CHAPTER 24

Nigel had been fortunate to never experience *genuine* hunger. Sure, there were lean times, when his father was ill, where he only ate one meal and a small snack, but he and his siblings never truly wanted. Those times helped frame Nigel's appreciation and gratitude for what he had and steeled him for tougher times.

Like now.

The Beefeaters didn't make it a priority to feed him. He fell asleep waiting, and they brought a small dish of leftover beef around midnight.

The bread on the plate was very hard and the beef tasted like it had been sitting out all day. Still, not knowing when he would eat again, Nigel ate as much of it as he could stomach.

To further complicate matters, the guards woke him up just before dawn the next morning. At first, he thought they were just being loud, but they specifically came by his cell, making noise to keep him up. When he inquired why, they muttered something unintelligible, and walked away.

Just after sunrise, Carlisle stood at the front of his cell, obscuring any light from the hallway.

"Up and at 'em," the warden said.

"What is the meaning of this?"

"Yours is not to question me in my prison," the warden said. "Now move."

Beefeater did not move, so Nigel had to step around him. When he did, the warden lowered his shoulder, forcing Nigel against the wall. He hit with an 'oof!', his shoulder digging into the hard stone.

"Move it!" the Warden said, grabbing his right arm, and pulling Nigel along. Pain shot up his right arm, causing Nigel to wince. He would not give the head Beefeater the satisfaction of hearing his discomfort, so he kept to himself.

It surprised him to discover that the prison workers took him back towards the middle of the prison, away from the bowels. Not only did it smell nicer, but this filled Nigel with hope this ordeal would it be short-lived.

In the back of his head, Nigel told himself to expect the worst. As if on cue, the Warden stopped middle of the hallway, moving past the Royal Family, the peasants.

"Wait here," Carlisle said.

"For what?"

Carlisle raised a hand, backhanding Nigel across the face.

"Silence!"

Nigel's eyes would have bored into Carlisle's soul if he had one. If it moved the older man, he didn't let it show. The warden turned on his heels and marched away.

After a handful of heartbeats, Nigel exhaled and leaned against the wall. He chalked it up to attempts at breaking him, but Nigel's pride would not have it. Nigel contained his anger, leaning against the wall with crossed arms, as if it were all a trivial joke. *If you're going to take me out, it won't be with these tactics.*

He thought he smelled lavender in his nostrils, and it reminded him of Ivy. *My darling wife. I cannot imagine what you must be feeling at this point.*

Nigel shook his head. Ivy was no delicate flower, and she would no doubt have the stomach to weather this storm. The timing couldn't have been worse, though, especially with her father's insistence that he keep his job. And Minnie, she had her entire future in front of her. Who would care for her if he stayed locked away? And there wouldn't be anyone to help her if her activities were discovered. And what that would mean for Charles...

He shook his head, disallowing that train of thought. Nigel looked to the ceiling, using the time to inspect for any weak areas he could use to escape. His body tensed up, expecting Carlisle or one of his accomplices to emerge and deliver a blow. Nevertheless, he refused to grant them the satisfaction of witnessing his fear.

A knot of unease settled in Nigel's stomach as he tried to act casual. The smell of meat and alcohol assaulted his nostrils. Nigel whipped around and immediately stepped back, assuming a defensive crouch.

Newsboy Cap stood over him, fists balled in a rage.

"Hello," Nigel said. The man's smile was the antithesis of friendly as he took a giant step forward. Nigel saw his eyes partially shut, bruises all over his face. He flexed his arms muscles, and his biceps were as big as Minnie's head.

Newsboy Cap raised his arms, his left in front of the right, fists still balled tight.

Even better: he's a pugilist and he's pissed at me, Nigel thought.

"Don't suppose you fancy a chat?"

Newsboy Cap grunted and took a swing at Nigel, who ducked and rolled out of the way. The large man's fist hit the stone wall, sending dust and debris flying. Nigel jumped to his feet and punched Newsboy Cap square in the spine.

The crack that followed came from Nigel's body. He groaned aloud, pain coursing up his arm. He didn't have time to contemplate the pain, as Newsboy Cap fired off two jabs. Nigel avoided the first, but the second got him in the chin.

He fell back onto the ground, breath leaving his body and his vision blurred. Now his opponent was a white blob coming at him. While Nigel retreated, his attacker quickly closed the distance. Lifted off the ground, Nigel felt the thick hands squeeze his throat. Despite Nigel's vision improving, Newsboy Cap remained unclear to him.

What wasn't coming was air. Nigel's throat tightened as Newsboy Cap squeezed. Grabbing the man's large meat hooks was a futile gesture, Nigel learned, as was punching or pinching.

Newsboy Cap pushed Nigel against a wall, air even more at a premium now. Instead of clearing up, black formed at the edges of Nigel's vision. In desperation mode, he kicked, punched, anything to keep fighting.

His foot connected with a soft part of Newsboy Cap, who eked out a whimper and dropped Nigel. Shaking his head, he could see the large opponent a bit more clearly. He was on his knees, hands clutching his privates. Taking advantage, Nigel sprinted toward his opponent, lowering his shoulder into Newsboy Cap's head. The force carried him into the wall. Uttering a battle cry, Nigel repeated the action two more times until the large man fell unconscious.

Nigel fell to the floor. He took deep, slow breaths to allow air to hit his lungs. He was sore and felt it as he stood again.

Newsboy Cap was out cold, but not wanting to chance a quick recovery, Nigel straightened his shirt and headed toward the upper level of the prison.

***

Warden Carlisle sipped a fresh cup of tea, dipping a scone into it. Crumbs fell onto his white puffy collar, but he didn't notice. Today was a good day, as he'd play a part in eradicating a traitor of the crown. It earned him a future favor from the nobility, which he hoped to parlay into a bigger pension. Retirement, after all, isn't cheap.

Carlisle closed his eyes, enjoying the pleasant silence that mid-morning tea afforded. His office was tiny for a man of his station, but it was almost twice as large as the average inmate's. The quiet gave him time to relax.

It didn't last long. A commotion erupted, probably a royal not getting enough beef or milk. But it didn't abate, like normal. It grew louder, getting closer. Carlisle groaned, slamming his teacup on his desk. He walked outside to see two of the more senior members of the Beefeaters – both in age and years of service – attempting to hold Nigel Barrington at bay, who, to Carlisle's consternation, was alive, and save for some scars, no worse for the wear. Nigel's eyes fixed on the warden, shooting daggers. He raised his hand, and the Beefeater allowed Nigel passage.

"Your plan failed," Nigel said, in a lower voice than Carlisle expected, but was no less thankful for. "I want my barrister, and I want him now."

To Carlisle's surprise, Nigel got legal representation fastidiously, and arrived within an hour of receiving a call. Apparently, his case was fast-tracked. Men in the employ of Her Majesty weren't allowed to languish. The warden instructed the Beefeater to stand guard, and if Nigel attempted escape, use whatever force necessary to bring him down.

No one made an escape attempt, and the barrister left, and Nigel returned to his cell, acting like a proper inmate. Frustrated, Carlisle informed an underling he was leaving early.

His modest home near South Kensington was empty. Carlisle's wife was still in Manchester visiting her sister and great nephew, and she put their servant on holiday. "You're old enough to fend for yourself," she told him. Carlisle felt a surge of gratitude, thankful that he could conceal his foul mood.

He walked into the kitchen, looking for the bread. He lifted the bread box when a voice behind him said, "Evening, Warden."

Carlisle gasped, and the bread box lid fell on his knuckles, prompting a loud groan. He turned to see a thin man in a loose-fitting suit sitting at his kitchen table. The man crossed his legs, resting his spindly fingers on his laps. The man was gaunt. The warden thought he looked like a walking ghost.

"Mister Drogo, to what do I owe this visit?"

"Our problem has not gone away," Drogo said in a quiet, raspy voice.

The warden swallowed hard. "I can still-"

"You failed, Warden Carlisle."

"See here, Mister Drogo. We can-"

Before Carlisle could blink, Drogo leapt from his chair and covered the distance between the table and bread box. Drogo's hands tightened around the warden's neck.

"The penalty for failure is death," Drogo whispered. Carlisle gripped the man's arm, but he was old, and out of breath. Despite Drogo's frail outward appearance, the man was muscular.

Carlisle heaved, trying to get air, but each attempt became more futile. He fell to one knee, his eyes pleading to Drogo for mercy. Drogo went about his task with the same indifference seen in opening mail or getting dressed. As black appeared around his vision, Carlisle wondered what could make a man so cold.

He hit the floor and the last thing Carlisle saw was Drogo smile, the few teeth he had rotting. His eyes closed for the last time.

***

"I can't believe this is happening so fast," Nigel said, buttoning his shirt. "Don't mistake that for a lack of gratitude. It's just astounding, is all."

"Lucky for you the barrister owed me a favor," Ivy said, smiling from the other side of the cell. "Father made the call."

Nigel's eyes widened.

"He called his top man, Barrister Entwistle. Turns out you impressed Father going to such lengths to save my life."

"He might end up liking me after all."

"If anything, you're good for business," Ivy said. "You're somewhat of a celebrity now, anyway. The trial of the century."

Nigel arced an eyebrow. "That so?"

"At least this week. All over the papers."

"Wonders never cease. Where's Minnie?"

"She's with Charles and my mother," Ivy told him.

"Your mother?"

"It would do no good for you to be acquitted only to face social disgrace by having your name sullied."

"Did I mention how much I love you?" Nigel asked, reaching for Ivy's hand.

"Not today."

Pairs of marching feet broke their joyful reunion up. Two Beefeaters marched to his cell, along with his barrister. It was time.

The courtroom was at capacity, and Nigel had to excuse himself in order to make his way through the waiting crowd. Going a mile a minute, and he felt the blood drain from his face.

"You didn't tell me to expect this," Nigel told his barrister.

"You know what's at stake with this trial."

Nigel looked at his Barrister, Jonathan Entwistle. He was in his mid-sixties, and the way he wore the wig looked almost natural on him. Nigel wondered if probably wore it at home, because he was bald underneath .

The man was one of Lovelace's most trusted friends and he took the case as a favor to Ivy. Nigel conveyed his appreciation many times. However, he wished he knew what to expect. The attorney for the crown, Hampton Winstead, entered the room. If Nigel didn't know any better, he could be Lord Rushforth's twin brother, save for the wrinkles and gray hair. He carried himself with an air of gravitas. People moved out of his way when he entered. He was a man used to getting what he wanted.

Not today, if Entwistle had anything to say about it. Sitting above him, was Rushforth, a couple more noblemen and a sickly looking man with long, thin fingers. The teeth he did have were rotting. Rushforth offered a smile, which was anything but pleasant. And being perched near the top was a subtle way of trying to assert what Rushworth considered his mastery over Nigel.

He found his wife and sister in the audience and smiled. Minnie returned the grin, resolve emanating from her face. Ivy, however, was unsure, fidgeting with her gloves. Not to worry her, he assuaged her with a nod of his head.

The bulk of the trial went by before Nigel knew it, his thoughts focused on his case. Entwistle had to nudge him twice to break him out of his stupor. Walking into the witness box, forcing himself to hold on to the sides to prevent his shaking being visible from everyone, especially Rushforth. He gave his testimony, having memorized it per his Barrister's suggestion.

After Nigel left the stand, Entwistle called his brother, Charles, to the stand. They were taking an enormous risk and doing this, given the nature of Charles's condition. Nigel was certain that his brother would not let him down or get him in trouble. His faith was rewarded, as his testimony brought forth hushed whispers and gasps from the crowd. The court had no choice but to side with the defense, and the crown's case was dismissed. Nigel turned immediately to Rushforth, whose scowl brought an inner joy. His men immediately got up and left, shoving people out of the way to do so.

He turned to look for Ivy, but she was not by Minnie. He looked at his sister, who shrugged. Nigel thanked Entwistle with a handshake and excused himself.

"Where's Ivy?"

"Someone came by and whispered to her, and she said her father needed her right away. That was fifteen minutes ago."

"We have to find her."

Minnie left the courtroom, taking Charles's hand. He asked some of the royal guards if they had seen her, but they had not. On the steps of the courthouse, Nigel saw his father-in-law standing there.

"Congratulations Nigel, I knew that this result would come about."

"Thank you, your support meant everything. Is Ivy with you?"

"No, she was in the courtroom with your sister."

Nigel's heart picked up its pace again. He explained what Minnie told him, and Lovelace's expression soured.

"I didn't need her for anything, other than to offer my support, which I did before she entered the courtroom."

Nigel asked Minnie and Charles to accompany Lovelace, while he went to call on someone. He decided this was a worse fate than being tortured in jail.

CHAPTER 25

Michael greeted Nigel with a handshake and pleasant smile at the front desk of the precinct.

"Didn't think I'd see you here, sir," Michael said. He leaned in and whispered. "Chief expected you to be convicted."

"I suppose it's in my nature to disappoint him," Nigel replied with a smile and looked at Lovelace.

"What can I do for you?"

"We're here to report a missing person: my wife."

"Oh my, sir. That's terrible." Michael's expression morphed into one of concern, but he was slow to move, as if caught.

"I'm sure you'll want as much information as we can provide."

"It's not that, sir, it's-"

"Michael, it's all right."

"The Chief has, well, barred you from the site, sir. We're to ignore you at best, or push any concerns to the bottom of the pile."

"Doesn't surprise me, Michael, and as a fine officer, I would never ask you to compromise yourself and your budding career on my account.

"But Mr. Lovelace is not only an admirable subject of Her Majesty, a titan of business, but also Ivy's father. And you would be well within your normal duties to consider this a request from him, I should think."

"Why, you are quite right, Inspector," Michael said, turning his attention to Mr. Lovelace. "Come with me, sir, and we'll see how we can help."

"Thank you," Nigel said. "Is Reginald here?"

"Don't believe so, but I've just gotten to the desk."

"I'll go look."

"Not a good idea, sir. Willoughby gave instructions."

"Understood. I would be in your debt if you'd pass a message to him, Nigel said, handing a folded note to Michael.

"Consider it done, sir."

Nigel nodded and turned to Lovelace. "I'm going to utilize other avenues on my end."

"Good luck, son."

Nigel watched as Lovelace walked with Michael. He smiled. *That's the first time he called me son.*

***

Minnie was sitting in the kitchen when Nigel arrived at home, compiling a list. Charles sat by her, making a cup of tea.

"You're both here, good. Charles," Nigel said, clasping his brother's shoulder. "Thank you so much for what you did today. I know what it meant for you, and yet you did it. It won't be forgotten."

Charles put a hand on Nigel's wrist. "Family."

Minnie saw this and forced out a gasp, tears streaming down her face. She mouthed the words 'He's never touched us like that before.'

The Barrington siblings took in the moment before Nigel stood.

"Work," Charles said, sliding the tea to Minnie and disappearing into his basement.

"I'm writing anything I can remember from court," Minnie said.

"I very much appreciate it. That will be very helpful," Nigel replied. "There's another favor I'm going to ask. Something that can be even more beneficial to our cause."

"Name it."

"I think your other hobby, as it were, would come very much in handy." Nigel said. "Would you be willing to resume it, post haste?"

With a smile, Minnie made for the stairs. "I thought you'd never ask."

"Can you please come here, brother? I require assistance."

Nigel knocked and entered Minnie's room. He stopped at the sight of her. Gone was her day dress, lying neatly on the bed. She wore the black dress with pink underneath, and matching riding boots. Minnie held a corset out toward him.

"Ivy and I work together," Minnie said, wanting to say more, but Nigel watched her snap her mouth shut.

Nigel took the corset, which had a bit of weight to it, and he remarked on that fact.

"Charles made them bulletproof for us," Minnie said.

"Well done," Nigel said, tying it. He thought he pulled hard, but if it bothered Minnie, she didn't say.

"Where did you plan on going first?" □

"Wadsworth. We've had good luck getting people to talk, so long as we didn't send them straight to hell."

"I'm sure you're very persuasive."

"That was all Ivy's doing. She makes this weird noise when she talks in the mask," Minnie said, pointing to the plague mask. "Sounds very evil."

"One of her many hidden talents," Nigel said, his thoughts turning to his wife and her warmth. *Hold on to that. Let it guide you to her.*

He tied the last of the corset, stepping away to admire his work. "All set."

"Not bad, brother. You might do okay if you have a daughter."

He smiled. "So how do we do this? Don't suppose we call a cab?"

"There is no we, dear brother. Unless you wish to don a dress and mask. I would think the grace of our Lord and Ivy's connections saved you from the gallows. I shan't think you wish to tempt fate again."

"Now see here, Minerva Jane. Not only am I your guardian until you are betrothed, but Ivy is my wife. And if you think I'm sitting here, leaving her fate to chance, you are sorely mistaken."

"I figured as much, and if you'd have let me finish, I told you I have a solution, but you may not like it."

She moved to her closet, reached into the back and pulled out a large wooden chest. It looked like one that Ivy used to keep her boots in. This one had a lock. Minnie pulled a pin from her hair and opened the box. She reached in, pulling out a mask.

The piece, made of solid brass, would be at home at a masquerade ball. The left eye was from a pair of goggles, while the right eye was a jeweler's loupe set inside a gear. There were two cogs on the forehead and one smaller one at the nose and mouth area, respectively. The back clasped together, but Nigel felt the heft in his hand and commented as such.

"I'm afraid there's no other option," Minnie said. "In the circle we are to travel, you're famous. Or, should I say, infamous. It's imperative that your face stay covered."

"Can't argue with you there. Charles made this overnight?"

Minnie chortled. "Heavens no. He's brilliant, sure. But I had him work on this after Ivy and I first went out. Thought maybe things would get to a point where you'd need to join us."

Nigel regarded his sister with a mix of pride and fear. Heaven help her husband, should he step out of line. "Don't tell me you gallivant around in that costume? Or did Charles make an invisible carriage?"

"Not quite," Minnie said, moving over to a chest at the foot of her bed. She lifted the lid and pressed a button in each corner. A secret compartment revealed itself, and a black cloak fell out.

"Most impressive," Nigel said.

"Watch this," Minnie said, pulling the cloak around her, backing up toward the shadows of her room. The only part of her that Nigel could see was her head and neck.

Minnie smiled, raising a finger. She opened the cloak, which was pink on the inside. She lifted flaps, exposing a small tool kit, machete and rope.

"As a lawman, I'd recommend you don't get arrested anywhere near a crime scene."

"Come brother, let's find Ivy and instill terror into the hearts of our betters."

Nigel worried that waiting for a cab would slow them, but Minnie telegraphed a request a half hour prior, so it was waiting for them when they went downstairs.

Nigel reached for his dark green coat, but Minnie chastised him. "You wear that all the time. You want to be inconspicuous, brother."

Nigel took the black coat, hiding the mask until he was in the cab and the horses began clopping.

The mask was a tad heavy, but the tie was sturdy, and didn't add undue stress to his head. At Minnie's suggestion, he twisted the gear around the jeweler's glass, and it magnified the view.

"Astounding," Nigel said, but his voice was off, as if he was yelling into a megaphone, but with static. "What the devil is this?"

"Charles called it a scrambler. You can talk, and no one suspects it's you."

"He thought of everything."

"That was my small contribution. Once I get us inside, you can have your fun."

"Once you get us inside?"

"Ivy and I have mastered our ability to get into places. I work my magic, you work yours."

"I can add forceful entry to your growing list of offences."

"Sod off. We're here."

The Wadsworth section was a prime example of the power of the British Empire. Old and new mingled as easily as immigrants to Her Majesty's home island.

But they weren't there to view the scenery. Minnie touched Nigel's arm. "Stand guard," Minnie said.

She turned her coat inside out, putting it back on. She covered the weapons with the flaps and put her mask on.

Nigel adjusted the mask again and nodded that he was ready. Minnie waved a hand, and they scurried down the adjacent alley. He noted landmarks just in case they'd have to return this way. Other than roughed up windows or an awning, most of the buildings were similar. No choice other than to trust Minnie on this one.

At the end of the alley, she motioned for Nigel to stop as two men passed. "Make haste," Minnie said, running across the street. Nigel did the same and they stopped under a large tree in front of the biggest home on the block. Its yard could hold a half-dozen homes.

"Whose residence is this?"

"Duke Beaufort," Minnie said, the bird-nosed plague mask garbling her words.

"I'm not sure I've heard of him."

"He hosts Rushforth and his men once a week, and they've made at least one business deal," Minnie said, trying to face her brother. "Beaufort's a skittish man."

Nigel could tell Minnie was smiling at that, even under the mask and followed her towards the home. There was a walkway with neatly trimmed shrubbery leading to the front, but Beaufort had gas lamps every few yards, so they stayed in the shadows. Minnie moved forward, head on a swivel. Nigel looked ahead, noticing the eight gas lamps near the entrance, four on each side in a crescent shape. He grabbed his sister's arm and pointed them out.

Minnie shook her head. "Servant entrance," she said, moving to the side of the Tudor-style mansion.

The door was closed, but candles were lit inside, and Minnie held up a finger. Nigel nodded and turned to keep watch as his sister gripped the handle. It opened, and Minnie tapped Nigel's arm.

They moved inside, only to find a man, carrying a butcher knife, walking toward them. He was burly, his forearms as wide as Nigel's thighs. His dark hair was a mess, and his apron had stains from the blood of the meat he cut on his arms and apron. He squinted his green eyes, and when he spied Minnie, lifted his knife.

"The bird demon!"

Before the words left his mouth, Minnie took the rope out, waved it above her head and hurled it toward the butcher. The man ducked, then watched as the rope hit the ceiling and fell a yard from his foot.

It provided the opening Nigel needed.

He stepped between the butcher and his sister, slamming his fist on the man's hand. Unprepared, the butcher dropped his knife. Nigel head-butted him. The butcher stumbled backward but didn't go down. Nigel head-butted him again and he hit the ground, unconscious.

He checked to see if the butcher had any keys on him, which he didn't. Nigel dragged the man up against the cutting table and followed Minnie upstairs.

The inside of the home was impeccable, and the furniture - no doubt heirlooms – as they are wont to be in the dwellings of the aristocracy – looked so clean they shone in the candlelight. Maps and pieces from India adorned the walls, and now Nigel knew where he heard the name of Beaufort: the family that helped get fellow subjects of the crown set up in the sub-continent.

He heard a cough, which seemed to come from behind the enormous wall in the foyer. The door was closed, but they could both hear someone muttering.

Minnie pointed to the door and raised three fingers. Nigel nodded as she counted down, then kicked the door open. The Barringtons went inside.

The Duke sat at a desk, poring over papers. An overweight fellow, his gray hair standing up, and his handlebar moustache needing a comb. His smoking jacket was open, and his rotund gut hung out over his vertically striped pants.

"What is the meaning of this?" He asked, his jaw dropping at the site of the costumes. "The demon!"

Minnie stalked right to Beaufort's desk. "Duke Beaufort, we need to talk."

CHAPTER 26

Beaufort stood, trying to back away, but his foot caught on his robe and he fell on his rear. Nigel heard a crunch, and Beaufort groaned as he grabbed his back.

"I'm sure we can work something out. I have hurt no one, I swear to God."

"You'll swear it to me!" Minnie yelled, walking right up to the Duke. Nigel took a spot over her right shoulder, blocking access to the desk and covering her from any reprisals.

Beaufort made a gesture and eked out a whimper. Even with the mask, Nigel could tell that the Duke needed a chamber pot.

"I'll talk, I'll talk! Whatever you want."

"Lord Rushforth," Nigel said.

Beaufort stiffened at the mention of his name. "W-what about him?"

"You may not be a killer, but we know he is. And he has accomplices. Are you an accomplice?"

Beaufort swallowed hard. "N-no."

Minnie produced the knife and held it above Beaufort's robust neck.

"No, please!" Beaufort whined.

"Answer!" Nigel demanded.

"I'll perish!"

"*I'll* kill you. Answer!"

Beaufort whimpered.

"It's not a murder, like ruffians on the street. It's a ceremony."

"What kind of ceremony?" Nigel asked.

"A ritual. We must follow the steps to open the door."

Nigel groaned. Beads of sweat trickled down his face. His face was getting hot, no doubt from the blood rushing to his head. "Enough with the riddles!"

Beaufort screamed. "It's Moldoreth! We're trying to usher in a new age with Moldoreth as our god. Rushforth has followed his teachings and used it to increase his wealth. Now, we're one sacrifice away from bringing about the god himself. We have to open the door from his world to ours."

"You killed those innocent women for a fairy tale!"

"They need to be pure, young and hair of gold to sate the beast."

"The married woman, Barrington, why take her?"

"Moldoreth will need a meal, as he has slumbered for eons."

"When is the last sacrifice?"

"They're securing the victim first."

"When?"

"I DON'T KNOW! I'm not privy to that information. I only know when the ritual is."

"Where?"

"It changes, in accordance with the moon. Usually it's in the temple."

Minnie leaned in, but Nigel put a hand on her arm. He knelt next to Beaufort, adjusting the jeweler's glass. Beaufort winced, his head moving back as the piece extended. For effect, Nigel tilted his head to the side.

He retracted the glass and turned to Minnie. "He speaks the truth."

"You're wise to be truthful, Beaufort."

"Thank you."

"We won't kill you...yet."

The Duke relieved himself, a puddle pooling under his leg. "What?"

"You will find out when the sacrifice is and where it was recovered from," Nigel said. "You will instruct your servant to place an advertisement in the Times, saying you're in need of a reliable mason, with the location being where the ritual is taking place. Is that understood?"

Beaufort nodded. "If Rushforth asks questions?"

"Believe me, if you fail us, whatever he does will be a mercy compared to what will befall you."

Minnie kicked Beaufort in the head, which hit the floor hard, knocking him out cold.

Minnie turned her coat around, making sure no one was watching. She stuffed her mask and gear in seconds, placing it in the small bag she folded into her pocket. Nigel tossed her the mask, which she hid as they walked toward town and the cab.

"And that's the Petticoat Society in action."

"Interesting name."

"We like it," Minnie said, shrugging.

Nigel's head felt like he'd dipped it in the Thames. He wiped it with a kerchief from his pocket and tried to wipe it away, but the kerchief became just as wet.

It's not the mask. It's Ivy.

He took a deep breath, trying to calm himself.

"Can you call on Reginald?" Minnie asked.

"I could, but we're not going to."

Minnie stopped in her tracks. "You must be lightheaded. We should get you some water. Because I think you just said-"

"There's nothing Reginald can do at this hour," Nigel said. "And even an excellent inspector like him could only do so much with opposition at the top. Not to mention that Rushforth is in his pocket.

"We're going to need evidence to get any of help from the police. And it'll be too late for Ivy."

"You think Beaufort will keep his word?" Minnie asked.

"He's timid, and was worried more about trying to maintain control of his bodily functions than trying to discern our identity.

"And since we found him at home, I think he's got no choice. He won't tell Rushforth," Nigel continued. "That man's just as likely to harm Beaufort's family and friends as he is the Duke himself."

"You've seen the girls," Minnie said. "Even if we can turn one or two like Beaufort, who knows how many there are. We're both skilled, but we're not equipped to take on four-to-one odds."

Nigel waived a cab and helped his sister inside.

Once settled, Nigel took one last look toward the direction of Beaufort's house. "Interesting choice of words, back there. Equipped. We have someone who can help with that."

Minnie smiled. "Charles is one man, and he's not one to share methods or instruct us."

"No, but he's likely to have parts of discarded projects we can put to good use."

"You know as well-"

"Minnie, believe me, I understand you're practical and prepared. I appreciate it. But I need something to maintain hope, that I can save my wife from something that could make the devil blush, which I may be powerless to stop."

They sat silent for a moment. "I didn't mean to upset you, brother."

"You're doing more than necessary to assist me. I am proud to have you as my sister."

Minnie squeezed his hand and held it for a moment. "We've taken what life's tossed us and come out better. I know we will this time."

Nigel smiled back at her. We're going to have to, Minnie. I cannot bear to lose Ivy."

Nigel and Minnie sorted through the three bins of scraps that Charles provided for them. He always let his siblings into the lab to look around, but not today. Nigel saw two large pages of drawings that Charles scribbled through and crossed out.

Minnie found a handful of small brass spheres. Nigel tied them into a pillowcase. "Good for a club."

"I like this new Nigel."

"Pray he never has to come out again."

A buzzing noise filled the air, prompting Minnie and Nigel to freeze in place.

"What is that?"

"Door," Charles said, going back to his drawings.

Nigel walked upstairs, finding Reginald at the door. "I came over as soon as I heard."

Nigel let him in. They sat in the living room.

"Michael told me what you suggested. Willoughby asked Michael to personally handle it. I'm too close to you, according to the chief. But I'm making personal inquiries in my spare time, which has just become scarce."

He produced a small notebook, and took out a daguerreotype photo of a rotund, well-dressed gentleman. Reginald turned it around so Nigel could get a better look.

Nigel kept his face neutral. "Who is that?"

"That is Duke Beaufort, found dead this morning. Being a close business associate of Rushforth, it's a top priority."

"Of course. They've got you chasing, what, three cases now?"

Reginald nodded. "But this one might have something the others don't: a justifiable lead. His servant heard him whispering about a bird lady."

Nigel chuckled. "I've been told the upper crust have their eccentricities."

"I'm not sure this behavior is eccentric. Earlier in the night, someone claimed to have seen a bird lady in a pink dress near Beaufort's chateau."

"I'm sure. Remember the calls we'd get about the red-eyed demon in the alleys of Wentworth?"

"I sure do. Those were a doozy. I also recall the Spring-Heeled Jack sightings, which turned out to be true."

"Are you saying this Bird Demon is real?"

"At this point, Nigel, I have to consider it. The pressure is getting intense to solve these."

"And no progress on the case of the missing girls."

The friends let those words linger for a few moments. Reginald rose.

"You've got your hands full with Ivy. I've got my ears open and have made a couple of inquiries."

"Thank you very much for that."

"I hate to ask a favor."

"Anything, my friend."

"We're canvassing dress shops for this bird lady's outfit. Would you happen to have the name of the dressmaker your wife and sister patronize?"

Nigel felt the blood drain from his face, but hoped it wasn't evident. "Let me ask Minnie. She's downstairs with Charles."

Minnie was still knee deep in the bins when Nigel approached and told her what Reginald asked.

"You think he's on to something?"

"No, I think he's starting out where he can. But we must be careful."

Minnie handed Reginald the name and Nigel saw him out. Once gone, Minnie collapsed in a chair.

"Well, there goes that. Without Beaufort, we're lost," Minnie said looking up at her brother. "I'm sorry, poor choice of words. You don't suppose we were too hard on him?"

"That was tame by police interrogation standards," Nigel replied. "My guess is his death was not because of natural causes."

"You think someone else killed him?"

"I know it. We should not give up hope yet. I know someone who might be help."

***

Nigel got out of the carriage about a half mile from Ainsworth's home. He wasn't sure what kind of reception he'd receive and figured the fewer people that saw or heard it, the better. Lovelace's kindness shone through as he offered to foot the bill for all expenses in the search for Ivy. Nigel seized this opportunity and used their generosity to arrange for a carriage for the evening, even treating the coachman to a satisfying meal that included a well-deserved ale.

Unlike the other members of nobility, Ainsworth lived in a Regency-style townhouse. Because of higher land prices in towns, even large houses tended to be built upwards on long, narrow plots. While connected to other buildings, giving it, from far away at least, appearing to be just another row home, Nigel knew better. There was likely a coach house, stable block and quarters for the servants. Giving him ample room to hide if need be.

Nigel no longer suspected Ainsworth of anything other than keeping evil company, a thought he kept at the fore as he knocked on the door.

An older, yet still stout, butler answered the door. His wide arms and shoulders stretched the limits of his tuxedo coat. Looking at his white hair and wrinkles, Nigel pegged him to be roughly as old as Lovelace, early sixties.

"May I help you?" He asked, a hint of vitriol in his voice.

"To whom do I have the pleasure of addressing?"

"Dodson."

"Well, Dodson, I am Nigel Barrington, here to see the Lord Ainsworth." Nigel produced his card.

"You are that inspector," Dodson said.

"I'm here on a social call. I am hoping his Lordship would look past our recent...difficulties for a few minutes of his time. It's a matter of life and death."

Dodson looked over the card, then scrutinized Nigel. "Wait here," he said, closing the door in his face.

Nigel huffed and turned around, clasping his hands behind his back. Since their tête-à-tête at the station, and subsequent meetings, Nigel wasn't sure how close an eye Rushforth kept on his associates. A few people were out tonight, mostly dressed for work at the factories. Some headed to or from an evening of entertainment. The window next to him and across the street had some candlelight, but he didn't see anyone in silhouette. Nigel took a deep breath, just as the door opened.

"His Lordship will see you."

"Excellent," Nigel said, following Dodson inside. The doorway opened into a massive foyer, with bookcases built into the wall and the solid walls adorned with tapestries. Dodson took Nigel up a small flight of stairs and turned around, where Ainsworth pored over documents at an ornate rolling desk, replete with carvings of Roman gladiators.

Nigel walked in, puffing his chest and standing as tall as he could, but he relaxed as Ainsworth looked at him. He forgot the young lord was smaller than him without wearing the boots of Spring Heeled Jack.

The craftmanship of the desk, caught the Inspector's attention, so much so that Dodson coughed to get his attention.

"May I present Nigel Barrington."

"Thank you, Dodson."

"Your Lordship, thank you for seeing me on short notice."

"I see your manners have improved outside the police station. I am not accustomed to taking visitors at this hour, but I figured by granting you this favor, we'd consider all debts paid."

"An excellent notion. I come here tonight no longer as an Inspector, but as a humble subject of her Majesty, who could use your insight in a situation I believe you are familiar with.

"My wife, Ivy has gone missing. I have it on good authority that the late Duke Beaufort, of which I believe you are acquainted, knew of her whereabouts, and was to share them with me."

"You get fired from the police force and turn to conjecture?"

"I'm going to speak freely. We both know you're connected to Rushforth, whether or not you want to be. I know he has a hand, somehow, in my wife's disappearance. I'm not here to make waves. The goal is to get her back.

"You've lost family, and I believe you to be an honorable man." Nigel stepped forward and got down on his knees. "Please, Lord Ainsworth, I just need to know where he gathers for his rituals. I'll blame it on Beaufort. But please, help me find my wife."

CHAPTER 27

Ivy's eyes flew open. She felt groggy, seeing double. She shook her head and attempted to lift it, but it was encased in some sort of headgear, preventing movement. Her fingertips tingled, and rivulets of sweat snaked down her forehead.

The tingling was sharp, and she wriggled her wrist in response, but it didn't move. Someone shackled her to a stone table. Ivy felt the cold envelop her. Lifting her head as far as she could, Ivy noticed she was in some sort of church. The stone she was on sat above a small altar. Two candles were lit above her and at the far end of the room.

She was alone, and considered screaming for help, but a heartbeat's pause made her reconsider. *I am here for a nefarious purpose, and I would wager one guess who put me here.*

Her heart raced, and rather than allowing it to accompany panic, Ivy thought of the Petticoat Society. That made her feel powerful, and that power helped take down important men. Now, it would free her, and get her back to Nigel.

She tried lifting her arms higher to see if her hands could touch, but they were too far apart. Her feet were also shackled, but she could move herself towards the top of the table, albeit a few inches. That didn't loosen the shackles.

The restraints were made of leather. *They can be broken.* Despite her fatigue, she tugged as hard as she could, lifting her legs as high as possible, pain exploding in her thighs. Ivy emitted a faint groan, her efforts were in vain.

A loud creak broke up the silence, echoing all around her. Lifting her head, she made out the outline of a dark shadow moving toward her. Ivy's eyes widened. *Am I to meet a veritable demon?*

She exhaled as the mass moved closer. It was a man in black robes, a hood and mask covering his face. As the man slinked toward her, she could see a beard sticking out the bottom of the mask. Ivy felt the man's piercing eyes on her. She met them and knew at once who this was.

"Rushforth, you bastard."

"Such impropriety, Mrs. Barrington."

"You're not worthy to say that name."

"Soon, you will bear witness to a greatness beyond comprehension, something I've been waiting for my whole life. I will accomplish what my father and grandfather could not: transform the world."

"I won't help you do anything but die," Ivy retorted, spitting at him.

Rushforth laughed as he wiped the spittle away. Reaching into his robe and pulled out a kerchief.

"You're very feisty, something the master will savor. But it won't do any good to have all the fight out of you before he arrives."

Rushforth moved the kerchief toward her face. Ivy smelled something sweet, like honey, followed by a smell that reminded her of household cleaning products. Rushforth put it over her mouth. She shook, screamed and tried to bite it, but no avail. Within seconds she felt her eyes get heavy, and she fell unconscious before they closed shut.

She struggled to keep her eyes open and after whispering protest, she passed out.

— ❖ —

CHAPTER 28

Nigel leapt from the folding step of the carriage before it came to a halt in front of his house. He thrust the door open and ran inside, causing Minnie to run toward him.

"Good heavens," Minnie said. "It's not like we don't have enough to make us feel faint!"

Nigel stopped in his tracks, narrowing his eyes. "What are you-"

"Thank goodness, Nigel," Lovelace said, his booming voice filling the open foyer. He came around the corner, his tie undone and hair standing on end.

"I wasn't aware you were stopping by."

"Forgive my unannounced visit," Lovelace said. "My wife and I were wondering if you had some news on Ivy?"

"We have our best lead yet."

"Thank the maker," Lovelace said, loud enough to make Minnie jump. "I can call on -"

"Reginald is calling upon his finest colleagues to assist us," Nigel continued.

"Then I will take my leave and let you get to it," Lovelace said.

Nigel turned to Minnie. "Can you retrieve my satchel? The one we worked on earlier?"

"Of course," she said, bowing toward Lovelace and running to Charles's lab.

"My son," Lovelace said, clasping Nigel's shoulders. "Bring our dear Ivy home."

"I will, sir." *Or die trying.*

***

Minnie and Nigel sat in the carriage, clad in their Petticoat Society getups.

"Where are we going?"

"Ainsworth gave me the address of an old yachting club that Rushforth owns. He's had the building shut down for two years, but Ainsworth said some of his less public activities carry on there. He said it's a logical a choice as any."

"And you didn't have to injure Ainsworth? He volunteered this information?"

Nigel nodded. "I appealed to his sense of familial loss."

"And Reginald?"

"I had to say something for Lovelace to back off. Securing Ivy's safety helped seal it." Nigel grinned. "I didn't become a good copper on my looks and stature alone."

Minnie smiled back, then looked out the carriage window. "Tonight's the night, according to Beaufort. What if she's not there?"

"We'll find her. No matter what. She's out there. I must hope that. Otherwise, she is lost."

Nigel had the driver stop the carriage three blocks from the address Ainsworth gave him, instructing him to park near the comfort of darkness in an alley. Minnie got out and moved toward the shadows, unbuttoning her cloak as she did so. Nigel asked the driver to wait and composed a quick note.

"Nigel!" Minnie whispered.

He shushed her with a finger to his lips as he placed the note in an envelope. Nigel gave it to the driver, along with a small sack of coins.

"Please take this note to the address on the envelope. I added an extra sixpence to your fee. And go back the same way you came." *I'm not taking any chances with my beloved's life.*

Minnie stepped out of the shadows, securing the mask onto her face. Nigel buttoned his coat, and Minnie retrieved his mask from the inside of her jacket. He donned it and walked out of the alley, carrying the satchel.

Fortunately, the streets were quiet. Most of the overnight workers started their shifts, and many second shift workers were already in the pub or at home. They shuffled through the gas lit areas, hugging shadow as best they could.

After a couple of blocks, the residential area gave way to a building zone. Every second or third building was in a state of disrepair – windows boarded up, exterior missing paint. Those sat around homes that looked like the paint had just dried and the construction crews had just packed up their tools that morning. Nigel thanked a higher power that this job didn't have a third shift.

Ainsworth told Nigel to look for a grounded steeple, and sure enough it was sitting in the bed of two large carts at the end of the next block. When Nigel asked how Ainsworth knew this, the noble said Rushforth talked of run-down properties he had recently purchased. Ainsworth thought it odd, though not nearly as much as jumping around London in a homemade costume, so he let it go. Nigel motioned for Minnie to pick up the pack, and to her credit, she did.

"It's just ahead, past the steeple," Nigel said. "Be on guard. If I were Rushforth, I'd set traps."

"But you're not an arrogant ass," Minnie retorted. "I think he's too full of himself to worry about people figuring him out."

Nigel had to admit that not only made logical sense but would be exactly what Rushforth would do. "Still," he said, reaching into his satchel, "Best be prepared."

He pulled out a pistol. While he surrendered his police issue revolver upon suspension, he purchased one for home to protect the women in his life. He didn't expect that he'd have to use it.

They rounded a corner past the spire, and the building in front of them was not like the others. This one was complete, with marble columns, a clock – its rusted hands stuck at eleven and nine – in a steepled tower at the top, and Greek and Roman figures around the clock. Nigel could not see any signs of distress or disrepair, despite the windows being boarded up and a *Do Not Enter* sign covering the door.

"Would you wager mother's pearl hairbrush that Rushforth owns the buildings around this one?" Nigel asked.

"C'mon, let's find a way in."

"I'd say the front door," he replied.

Minnie nodded and moved to the front door. She put her hand on it and waited. Nothing happened.

Nigel moved his gloved fingers around the edges. "Not affixed to the frame. Cover me, I'm going to move it."

He pulled from the left, thinking the door handle would be on that side. The sign moved but didn't come off. In fact, it barely moved.

"I say."

"Here," Minnie said, pointing to the right side. "There are large bolts keeping it tied down."

"There may not be any traps," Nigel said, "But I bet if we move these, it will give our position away."

"I concur, but what choice do we have?"

"Come here," Nigel offered. "I'll pull this open as far as I can. You get in and push from the inside, so I can get through."

Minnie nodded and took her place next to him. Nigel grabbed the door, looked at his sister, who raised a finger.

Nigel pulled. He dug in his boots, pulling as far as he could. He winced, feeling his muscles ripple and strain. Minnie ducked under his arm and walked inside.

He felt an unseen force give him a boost, pushing the barrier out an extra foot. Holding onto the door, Nigel shifted the position of his hands, so he could join Minnie. There was no door on the other side, so Nigel stepped into the door frame. He reached out and pulled the satchel in behind him.

"I'm in," Nigel said. Minnie let go of the barrier as Nigel eased it back into place.

"That wasn't a wide opening," she said. "For once, I'm glad I have a corset on."

Nigel shook his head as he opened the satchel. "Let's find my wife."

The corridors were empty, a good thing since some items in the satchel echoed in the cavernous area upon hitting the ground. They couldn't fashion much, but Nigel hoped it was a case of every little bit helps. Minnie fashioned a mace with old brass parts, while Nigel constructed a Gatling-style projectile launcher that hurled cogs and gears. Charles added a leather strap, and Nigel mentally thanked his brother as he slung it over his shoulder. Minnie clipped her mace to her belt and nodded. Nigel led her down the dark hallway.

The air was ripe with the smell of rotten apples permeating the filters of Nigel's mask. *Rushforth must not have sent ye royal housekeepers to this establishment in a while.*

He stopped at the end of the hallway. "Where are we going?" Minnie asked.

"Left," Nigel said, turning in that direction. The smell disappeared, but this corridor had pockets of darkness, which cause the hair on his neck to stand on end. Who knows what impediments awaited?

Best to remember Minnie's words: he's too arrogant to think you'd find this place.

Nigel's inner voice whispered caution, urging him to remain alert. Though dark, Moonlight crept into the hallway through a small stained-glass window, and Nigel followed the beams of light as best he could. He chanced a peak at the icons on the windows. They contained Stations of the Cross, which meant this was once a church, or had them imported from a church into this house of business. *I wonder if the Almighty would appreciate the irony.*

Nigel knew his steps were exaggerated, and he looked around. A lot of things could hide in the darkness. *And given the darkness Rushforth is up to, I must stay vigilant.*

He looked ahead to Minnie. She had proven capable of taking care of herself, but that was against one man, who was stronger than Nigel. *Am I tempting fate by bringing her here? I appreciate her help in bringing my love – and a woman she loves as a sister – home.*

I cannot lose them both. But I will lose Ivy without help. And right now, I can rely on Minnie. And if you cannot rely on family, then a man will have a hardscrabble life.

There were no traps in the darkness, and at the end of the hallway, Nigel turned right, where firelight guided the path. Minnie followed him, and he picked up the pace.

The lights grew brighter, and Nigel was almost into a sprint as he saw them. The hallway opened into what was once an enormous cathedral. Many of the rows of pews were gone, but the ones near the back were still intact. Nigel motioned for Minnie to join him there, and they knelt in front of the last row.

Eight men gathered around an altar, with a young girl, clad in white, tethered to it. Ahead of the near, near the far wall, lay Ivy, tied to a large stone slab.

It took every fiber of his willpower to not rush after Ivy, freeing her and carrying her away from his nightmare. Pain shot through his chest, which forced him to fall to his knees.

The men were chanting, and the woman whimpered, and he heard her beseech them to let her go. Nigel turned to Ivy, who appeared to be sleeping.

Minnie grabbed his arm. "What are you doing?" She whispered, which sounded more like a hiss through the mask. "Get her!"

"Look around. Outnumbered four-to-one, and they are all likely armed. As much as I want to go in here and end Rushforth, we need to be logical about this."

Minnie groaned and stood up.

Nigel took her arm and pulled her back to the ground. "You go over there, you condemn Ivy to death."

Minnie looked at him for a few heartbeats. "Then what are we going to do?"

"We have to split up, get their attention so we can free both women."

Nigel surveyed the scene. The low chanting stopped, which made the girl's whimpers on the altar even more heartbreaking. Rushforth stood up and turned to the robed figure at the base of the altar. He reached into his robe and produced a knife.

"Brother, you have proved yourself loyal to the cause. The Patriarchal Cross is stronger by your actions. You have earned the right to bask in our achievements and reap the benefits that follow.

Join us, take your place at our side. Spill the blood of the virgin and become one."

The rest of the brothers parted and the figure at the back stood there for a moment. He was bigger than the rest of the gathered group, and his reticent footsteps still echoed in the room.

The rotund figure took his place next to Rushforth, looking at the girl on the slab, then at the nobleman. He moved his hand to take the knife, but evidently didn't move fast enough, as Rushforth shoved the handle into his hand.

"Join us, brother," Rushforth said, standing behind the man. The others gathered began chanting *join us.*

Ivy lifted her head,

Nigel turned to Minnie. "Get Ivy. Go in the shadows, stay hidden. Don't move to her until you hear my signal."

"What's the signal?"

"You'll know."

Minnie regarded him. The chanting grew louder, more frantic. "Go," Nigel said, an edge of panic in his voice.

Minnie took off, and Nigel aimed his pistol.

He got the sights set on the would-be assailant's hand. Nigel took a deep breath, settling himself further.

Then, Rushforth did something Nigel didn't expect: he removed the fat man's hood.

Chief Willoughby, sweating profusely, lifted the knife above his head, as the young woman below him screamed.

CHAPTER 29

Nigel lowered his gun. He shook his head and used the monocle feature of his mask to zoom in. Sure enough, it was Willoughby.

Bloody hell. The Chief is part of this! Now his actions since Ainsworth's capture makes sense.

He saw a blur of pink out of the left lens of the mask. Following it, he watched Minnie across the room, crouched behind the slab, trying to undo Ivy's restraints.

The men's fevered chanting reached a crescendo. Nigel looked back at his former boss. The knife was still in his right hand, but it was shaking, getting worse as the pleas from his would-be sacrifice kept getting louder and more despondent. Willoughby put his left hand over the knife, steadying himself.

Nigel raised the gun, aiming it. He held his breath.

Willoughby exhaled, closing his eyes.

Nigel fired.

All hell broke loose.

***

The bullet roared out of the chamber, and the knife flew out of Willoughby's grip. He yelled and grabbed his hand as he fell to the floor.

"Blazes," Nigel whispered. "I meant that for his heart."

The rest of the men looked at Nigel, who stood, aiming for Rushforth, who picked up the knife and grabbed Drogo's arm.

"Finish the ceremony, we must have blood!"

Nigel fired again, and the gathered men scattered. He couldn't get a clear shot at Rushforth.

"After him!" Rushforth screamed. "It's but one man!"

Nigel aimed again. Click. "Blimey!"

Rushforth reached into his robe and pulled out a pistol. He fired, forcing Nigel to take cover as he reloaded. Spurred on by Rushforth, the rest of the Brotherhood moved toward the intruder.

Nigel reloaded and aimed again. Click. He cursed and looked at the gun. "It bloody jammed now!"

Dropping the gun, he opened the satchel and removed the pocket Gatling projectile launcher. He opened the top, took a bag of cogs and gears, dropping them inside. He closed it up and aimed at the oncoming members of the Brotherhood.

Chaos reigned around him. He gripped the handle for the wheel, waiting until the robed men were closer.

Two men crawled to the altar, chanting. Three more stood, running and looking for weapons.

"Don't suppose I could ask you to stand still," Nigel whispered to himself. □

He took a breath and turned the crank. The cogs and gears flew out, spinning toward the men. Despite being small, the metal parts made the men yelp in pain and surprise. One of them hit an oncoming member of the brotherhood between the eyes. His head flew back, and he fell to the ground, unconscious.

The rest of the men scattered, taking cover behind anything they could find to stay out of harm's way.

He wasn't visible at the moment, but Rushforth's screams were audible to all. He commanded his brothers to stay and persevere. It didn't have the effect the aristocrat hoped.

As he took this cue to work on the jammed rifle, Nigel looked up to see if his sister fared any better.

Minnie worked on cutting the straps holding Ivy down. Behind her, a figure stood over them. Nigel saw this and his eye widened, and his mouth dried out suddenly. He opened his mouth to scream, but nothing came out. Ivy's scream alerted Minnie to the attacker, Rushforth, who had a knife in his hand. He lifted it, but Minnie was fast. She turned and got up into a crouch. Rushforth sliced downward, but Minnie stood and kicked him and he fell off the slab.

She cut the strap holding Ivy's left leg down. Now that the brotherhood's attention was fully on Nigel, she moved to the front of the slab, working on the other leg strap.

Drogo stood over the other young woman, mumbling and waving his arms in large circles, ignoring the girl's pleas to stop. Nigel fumbled with the gun. *Curse my trembling hand! Lord, make it steady. I cannot bear to let another woman die when I'm so close to stopping it!*

He pulled the hammer, but it would only go back part of the way. Nigel looked up. The brotherhood was either recovering from injury or hiding.

His breath shortened and his heart threatened to eject itself from his chest. The drone of some brothers chanting, others yelling and looking for firearms. Nigel closed his eyes, took a deep breath, tuning out the noise.

Rushforth turned to see Drogo's progress and pointed to Minnie. "Stop her!"

Drogo opened his eyes and turned to see Minnie, now facing him. In what seemed like no time at all, Drogo was at the base of Ivy's slab, waving his knife at Minnie.

One brother used this distraction to charge. If he had kept quiet, no one would've known he was there. But the man yelled, and Nigel stood in time to swing the butt end of the rifle at him. The brother's mask shattered, and he was out cold before he hit the floor.

He felt adrenaline course through him as the attacker hit the floor. A police inspector usually liked to have suspects or witnesses. But when your boss was involved in the crime, and one's family was at risk, rules could be tossed aside to protect your loved ones.

Nigel worked on the gun, trying to keep an eye on Minnie. Drogo moved like a man closer to Nigel's age than a man near death.

Nigel gasped. He moved toward her, but his legs didn't move as fast as he wanted. They felt like they were shackled with iron. Sweat poured down his face. *Bloody hell! I have to be there for my sister! She is overmatched.*

He saw Minnie avoid Drogo's thrusts and slashes.

Over her shoulder, Rushforth took his place over the young girl and started chanting. □

Nigel screamed and slammed the rifle against the pew in front of him. He heard a click, checking the gun. The jammed bullet fell out. He aimed at Rushforth and fired.

The shot missed. Minnie kicked Drogo, and he fell into Rushforth, who moved in time to miss the bullet.

Nigel emitted a curse and moved from his hiding place. Rushforth turned, standing by Drogo, who looked ready to attack Minnie. Nigel fired again, and Drogo backed off, allowing his sister to parry Rush-forth's thrust.

For her part, Ivy was using all her limited strength to free herself.

"Hold on, love," Nigel whispered, pulling bullets from his pocket to reload the gun.

One brother rushed him. There were no jamming issues this time, and the shot hit the would-be attacker in the heart.

Minnie was holding her own against Rushforth, but the man has experience with hand-to-hand combat. Minnie did more dodging and ducking than actual fighting. Rushforth moved in, alternating be-tween stabs and slashes. Minnie's skirt had cuts in three places, but the leather petticoat had done its job.

Nigel fired a couple of shots at Drogo, and both he and Rushforth ducked. Minnie took the cue and moved up the slab, focused on the restraints of Ivy's left arm.

Two more brothers sped toward Nigel, looking to make it a group effort. *At least some of them are using their brains. Only a little.*

He fired, taking out the bigger of the two. Only one bullet re-mained, so he jabbed his assailant's stomach with the gun, then up-percut him. The brother stumbled back, and Nigel head-butted him unconscious.

Rushforth stood, small pistol in hand. Nigel ducked as two shots flew past. He looked up and Drogo had resumed the ritual.

Rushforth aimed at Minnie, and Nigel swore as fired. The noble-man had to dive out of the way.

Minnie freed Ivy's left arm and slid down the slab to take Drogo on. This provided a distraction for Ivy to continue working on her bonds. Ivy couldn't reach the right strap. She struggled, pulling her arm, then her body, as far to the right as she could, but it wouldn't budge.

Nigel only had one set of bullets left. He reloaded, aiming the gun at Ivy's slab, breathing to settle himself. Out of the corner of his eye, he saw a black mass move toward him. Nigel fired.

Ivy's arm was in mid-air when Nigel's shot hit the strap. Her momentum carried her body over to her left side and to the edge of the slab. She caught herself. Nigel's attention shifted to the approaching brother.

He whipped around, and it was Willoughby running toward him. Frozen, Nigel couldn't fathom why his former boss was still charging. *Must have been hiding on the ground or in a dark corner. Surprised he's not trying to save his life and run right out of here.*

Realizing his mask was on, Nigel readied himself for a fight. Anger swelled in him, and he felt his skin warm a bit as blood pumped through him. Tightening his hands into fists, he was prepared to pummel Willoughby.

But the Chief, clutching his injured hand, looked past Nigel toward the exit. He had no intention of fighting. *That's the smartest thing you've ever done, sir.*

Nigel moved back as Willoughby ran past. The chief didn't risk a look at his former subordinate. Nigel was thankful for that as he stuck his foot out. Willoughby fell, and Nigel stepped over him, punching Willoughby hard enough to knock him out.

Nigel ran toward the altars, but Rushforth fired a pistol in the air. Everyone froze.

"Hold it right there," Rushforth said, his face as red as blood. He aimed the pistols at Minnie and Ivy. "Another step and the women are dead."

He moved forwarded a few inches, but Rushforth fired at her feet and she stopped.

"Take off the mask," Rushforth said.

Nigel complied, holding the mask in his right hand. He looked at Drogo, who injected something into the woman on the altar, and continued chanting.

"Drop the mask. Now."

"You can't take all of us," Nigel said as he complied with Rushforth's demand.

"You do not know my capabilities. How else have I eluded you for so long?"

Minnie inched forward, and this time Rushforth fired, hitting her in the leg. Nigel screamed and moved forward, but Rushforth's next shot landed right at his feet.

"That was deliberate, Barrington." Rushforth raised the gun a few inches. "As will the next one."

Ivy used this time to move next to Minnie, trying to help.

"Not another step," Rushforth warned.

"She needs help."

"I care not. Another centimeter and you perish."

"You won't shoot me," Ivy said. "You need me for this show of yours."

"I just need you alive. That does not mean you can't be in pain."

Nigel used this time to move his foot forward, catching the back of the mask with the toes of his boot. While Rushforth bantered with his wife – good work, Ivy – he made sure he had the mask, and kicked it upward.

He grabbed it in mid-air with his right hand and spun. Rushforth turned his head, moving the pistol in his left hand.

Nigel hurled the mask, ducking and doing a somersault as Rushforth's bullet sailed harmlessly overhead.

The mask would not hit Rushforth, and he raised an eyebrow.

The mask hit Drogo, knocking him off balance.

Nigel crawled to a rifle, picking it up, firing the rest of the round. One of them grazed Drogo, and he fell beneath the altar. One hit Rushforth's robe forcing him to dive toward the slab.

When he landed, Ivy leapt at him. Rushforth recovered quickly, in time to see Minnie lunge for him. He swiped his knife at Minnie, cutting off the nose of her mask.

Ivy used the momentary distraction to leap at Rushforth, kicking the knife out of his hands. Minnie rushed in, attacking Rushforth's joints and throat, but he deflected the blows.

He backed into Drogo, in mid-cantation. The diminutive man groaned and reached into his robe, pulling out a pistol and aiming it at Ivy.

Nigel sprinted toward Drogo, leaping onto the altar and tackling him as his shot flew past Ivy.

"You!" Drogo spat, lifting the knife toward Nigel's throat. He backed up, and the gaunt man's knife sliced the top button off his coat.

Nigel elbowed Drogo's arm, expecting to hear a crack. Instead, his elbow throbbed as the skinny arm stopped the blow cold. *That can't be muscle. He's not much more than a skeleton!*

Drogo backhanded Nigel's chin, and stars entered his vision.

Nigel recoiled, pain coursing through his arm. Drogo slashed at him, but Nigel fell to the ground to avoid it, and he felt like his upper body was on fire.

Turning back to the slab, Drogo emitted a chant that ended with a yell. Kneeling, he sliced the young girl on the slab in three locations. She screamed as he did so.

Nigel got up, noticing the cuts were in the same spot as the other dead girls. Drogo muttered something to himself and got on his knees, eyes fixated on the blood leaking out of the girl's body.

Nigel ran towards the man, but instead of taking Drogo head on, he put his hands down on the top left corner of the altar, swinging his legs around. His feet struck Drogo in the back of the head, and the gaunt man's forehead hit the slab and flew back, unconscious before he hit the ground.

Nigel stumbled off the altar, his right hip hitting the ground with a thud. His teeth rattled, and pain roared in his mouth. Shaking it off, he stood and looked at the girl.

She was younger than Nigel thought, seventeen by his wager. *My word, she's a lot like Minnie was when Mother and Father passed.* Her face was red from crying, as were her wrists. She looked at him, her green eyes pleading for help.

"My name is Nigel. What's yours?"

"An-Angelique."

"That's a lovely name. Angelique, I'm going to get you out of here. I just need you to lie still for a few minutes, so I can free you from these shackles, okay?"

Angelique nodded, and Nigel unbuckled her left hand from the slab. Angelique immediately moved her hand to her cuts, and she hyperventilated. He produced a handkerchief from her pocket.

"Here, put this on your chest," Nigel said. "Apply pressure."

Nigel reached for her right hand, but he heard a gunshot ring out, followed by a muffled scream. He whipped around to see Rushforth's foot on what remained of Minnie's mask, and two guns in his hand: one trained on him, one on Ivy.

"Not another step, or we see who dies faster: you or your wife."

Nigel stayed still, putting his arms in the air. Behind him, Angelique sat up, and Rushforth pulled the hammer back on his pistol.

"That goes for you too, wench. Lie back on the table."

Angelique looked at Ivy, then at Nigel, who gave her a slight nod. She tried to lie down, but whimpered, moving the kerchief to her abdomen.

"Now."

"You said she has to be alive. She bleeds out, you lose."

Rushforth eyed him. "Quickly."

Nigel stood next to Angelique. He put his right hand in his pocket for a moment, before using it to provide support and she lied back, grimacing as she did so.

"There, there now," Nigel said, his eyes reverting to his pocket. Angelique squinted, a look of confusion on her face. He looked down again.

Angelique looked at the pocket, and Nigel smiled as her eyes widened. A small knife stuck out of the top. Angelique nodded and put her left hand on his pocket. "Bless you," she said, taking the knife, using the handkerchief to hide it.

"All right, Barrington. Now turn around, hands up."

Nigel complied, exaggerating his movement to allow Angelique more time to hide the knife against her body.

He spotted Ivy, who nodded, her eyes as fierce as ever. She's fine.

"I've done as you asked," Nigel said to Rushforth. "Now let my sister go."

"She is most aggravating, and if I let her up, I'm likely to blow her head off in anger. You're not in a position to ask for anything, in any event."

"I beg to differ. We seem to be deadlocked."

Rushforth laughed. "You amuse me. It's no wonder you couldn't figure out what was going on under your nose."

"I see all that money hasn't given you brains. You can shoot me, sure, but you'll have two very upset women to contend with. And your lackey is dead."

"Maybe I'll just take them out first."

"And that would be to your detriment, because I'll become the most dangerous creature alive."

"What's that?"

"A man with nothing to lose."

Rushforth smiled. "Your bravado is commendable, but the truth is, this will all be over soon. You see, we don't need to do anything with the wench over here," he said, gesturing to Angelique. "She'll just bleed out, and once the Darkness arrives, you'll be dead any way.

"Go on, try something foolish. It's preferable. You'll be thankful to be dead once the Lord Of all Night sees his meal," said Rushforth said, looking at Ivy.

Minnie used this distraction to punch Rushforth in the back of the knee. Rushforth groaned, and his arms moved, forcing the guns away from Ivy and Nigel.

They leapt at the nobleman. Rushforth tried to aim his guns. He fired, and Nigel felt a sharp pain rush through his right shoulder. His pace slowed, and he fell to his knees inches from Rushforth and Minnie.

CHAPTER 30

Nigel touched his shoulder. He looked down, the oozing blood saturating his gloves.

Sitting up, with his left arm to brace himself, he mentally cursed himself as pain enveloped his entire right side.

A shadow loomed over him, and Nigel could see the shadows arm go up, clutching something. He turned and Rushforth loomed over him, knife in hand.

Nigel rolled out of the way as Rushforth's strike came down, missing him by inches. The extra weight on his right arm caused an involuntary scream, but it sounded like a battle cry instead of weakness, so Nigel went with it. He kicked Rushforth in the stomach, allowing Minnie, who had removed her mask and carried her homemade mace, to leap into the fray.

She toyed with him a bit, twirling the makeshift weapon in the air to build momentum, then swinging high and low at Rushforth. Nigel tried to get up but felt a pair of hands under his arms. He tensed, until feeling they were soft and small.

"Ivy."

"Are you hurt?"

"Only when I move." Nigel looked at Minnie, continuing her elegant yet deadly dance with Rushforth. "We need to help her."

"She's stalling."

"Where are his guns?"

"He tossed one. Out of bullets. I think the other one is on his person."

Nigel grimaced. "We must take him down. He *cannot* escape."

"You are in no position to fight, darling."

"If he gets out of here, we're finished. Two and half against one are pretty good odds."

"I trust you have a plan of some kind?"

"Indeed, my dear," Nigel said, smiling. "I'm going to cater to his deepest, most fervent desire: taking my life."

Ivy helped Nigel up, and they checked on Angelique. She was holding steady, but blood still trickled out, her skin turning pale. Nigel asked for the knife, and she handed it over.

"Just hang on, as best you can."

She nodded. Nigel took the knife and slit Drogo's throat, to prevent any last-minute surprises. He shuddered after doing it, and Ivy squeezed his left arm.

"Let's end this," he said.

Minnie swung the mace and Rushforth ducked, and he looked miffed. When he stood, Rushforth stopped, smiling.

"This should be fun," he said, motioning for Nigel to attack, and he obliged, knife in his left hand.

Stepping forward, Nigel feigned high and slashed low, but Rushforth anticipated it. The noble gave him a look of amusement, but Nigel smiled, because Ivy rushed him from the right with a piece of the leather strap that held her to the slab. She connected on his exposed arm, and he groaned. Rushforth lifted the knife over his head and plunged downward, but Ivy was ready. She caught the knife with her strap and wrapped it.

Rushforth twisted the handle with his free hand. With the echoing of the metallic crank of turning gears, the Barrington siblings came to a stop.

As the knife handle expanded, a second blade emerged, completely enveloping the smaller one. Rushforth flicked his wrist as he closed the handle around the new blade.

Rushforth kicked Ivy in the stomach, tearing the strap apart like a piece of flimsy paper. She fell back.

Nigel yelled and advanced, rage overtaking his pain. Rushforth easily avoided his left-hand uppercut, punching Nigel in his wound. He howled as he twisted onto the ground.

Minnie fared no better, each swing of her mace parried. Rushforth ducked an attack meant for his head, slicing the mace and catching Minnie's forearm. She screamed and retreated, covering the wound.

Nigel pressed his attack, but Rushforth picked Ivy up, wrapping an arm around her neck. He reached into his robe and produced another pistol, jamming it against Ivy's temple.

Nigel froze.

Balling his hands into fists, Nigel looked at Minnie, who held her leg and grimaced, tears moving down her cheek. Nigel felt the blood rush to his head.

"Let her go. Shoot me, end this. I've been a thorn in your side since I caught Ainsworth. Enact your revenge."

"You are correct on all counts, Barrington. But I've no need to enact revenge." Rushforth looked at Angelique. "Once she's dead, Moldoreth will be here, and you will end."

Nigel laughed. "That's your brilliant plan? The genius Lord Rushforth is going to *wait?* I can't believe I deemed you a threat."

"Scoff all you want. I'd say goodbye to my loved ones, were I you. I estimate," Rushforth said, watching Angelique, "you have minutes left."

"You're delusional," Ivy said.

"Careful. You might anger me enough that I shoot you by mistake."

"Threaten her and-"

"You're in no position to do anything but *die!*" Rushforth took a moment to compose himself. "The wheel of progress moves forward, and every day, we have more mouths to feed. Riff-raff have more children, many of whom beg on the streets, bring disease, and steal from their betters. There is a reason that, throughout history, the strong have survived.

"It's no coincidence that families like mine have endured for centuries. Sure, some of you may have a generation or two do well," Rushforth said, whispering in Ivy's ear. "But a grandchild or great-grandchild will squander it, and you're on the street, begging, or getting sick. Today, Lord Moldoreth will end that. Only those that are *worthy* of surviving will."

"You're insane, if you think you can harness the power of the spiritual realm," Nigel spat. "Your money has brought you nothing but arrogance."

Rushforth laughed. "It's a wonderful quality to be amused in the face of death. I-"

A gunshot rang out and Rushforth's head flew back, blood gushing from the wound in his head. Ivy fell from his grasp, blood clinging to her golden hair.

Time seemed to slow down around Nigel as Ivy moved closer to the earth. With his mouth agape, he was aware of air escaping from his lungs, yet his scream remained unheard.

He ran to his wife, falling by her side just as she hit the ground, taking her in his arms.

"Ivy, darling, I'm here."

He watched her eyes flutter, then open, her breath coming in brief spurts. "Nigel!"

He picked up her up, squeezing her as tight as he could. "Thank the maker."

Ivy tapped him on the arm. "Can't...breathe."

Nigel pulled back, and Ivy put a hand on his cheek, kissing him. He smiled and took her hand.

"I thought my world just ended," Nigel said. "Are you hurt? Did you get shot?"

"No, it's all Rushforth's blood."

He kissed her again, only to be interrupted by a gun shot.

"Everyone, stay where you are!"

Nigel raised his arms and turned to see Reginald leading a squad of Her Majesty's Police force into the building.

— ❦ —

CHAPTER 31

"I was about to curse our driver," Nigel said, putting his arms down. "I was very explicit with my instructions."

"With Willoughby out, I had to go through proper channels," Reginald said, waving his arm and holstering his pistol. "They said it'd be morning before I'd get an answer, so I told 'em to sod off."

Nigel smiled. Behind him, Minnie squeaked, and he turned to see her trying to get up. Ivy and Nigel came to her side.

"How are you, sister?"

"I'll survive as long as I don't see you kiss anymore."

Nigel laughed. Ivy tore off the bottom ruffles of her dress, wrapping them around the wound. Reginald came over to them.

"Minnie, are you okay?" Reginald asked, then looked at Ivy. "Ivy, you too. Good heavens Nigel, what have you done to these women?"

Nigel and Ivy laid out what happened. Reginald folded his arms, as if waiting for more. Nigel looked at Ivy, who nodded. He laid out the story of Petticoat Society.

Reginald laughed. "I...I don't know what to say."

"Will you be arresting us?" Ivy asked.

"No, Ivy, I won't. The real instigators are gone, and based on the looks and you and Miss Barrington, well I think you're the victims in this whole affair."

Ivy exhaled. "Thank you."

"Your timing could not have been better," Nigel said. "I had Rushforth where I wanted him."

Reginald chuckled.

Ivy slapped Nigel's arm. "Waiting until your beloved has a pistol to her head to make a move? How you became an inspector is beyond me."

Reginald's chuckle turns into raucous laughter at this.

"Sir!"

Reginald turned around, and Michael stood there, his arm around Willoughby, who was in handcuffs. He swallowed hard, looking at the ground. "You said round up anyone in black, sir."

"I certainly did. Well done, Michael. Instruct the medical personnel to come in when they arrive, post haste."

"Aye sir," Michael said, letting Willoughby go, and the former inspector stood there, still holding his right arm. *He's paler than usual.*

"Are you injured, sir?" Reginald asked.

Willoughby shook his head. "You must understand, I was not part of this. That is to say, I was coerced against my will."

"You were a part of it, *sir*," Nigel said, prompting both Willoughby and Reginald to do a double take. "But one thing is true: you aren't intelligent enough to concoct a plot like this."

"We take that into consideration," Reginald said. He turned back toward Willoughby. "Out of respect for your station and what you've done for me, sir, I don't want to put shackles on you."

"Thank you, Reginald."

"Please don't make me regret that."

Willoughby nodded and turned around. Reginald gestured for him to go. He turned toward Nigel and whispered, "That was cold."

Nigel just shrugged.

Four men entered with Michael, all dressed in white coats and carrying leather bags. Ivy directed two of them, carrying a stretcher to Angelique. They took one look and got her loaded on one and out the door.

"Looks like you won't die, after all," Nigel said, stepping aside to let a doctor by. He was younger than the others, with a chiseled chin and warm, inviting blue eyes. He knelt next to Minnie, who smiled at on him.

"Hi, I'm Doctor Paddington. Let's see what we have here, miss..."

Minnie was silent for a heartbeat until Nigel cleared his throat. "Barrington. Minerva Barrington. Minnie."

"I'll fix you right up, Minnie."

She smiled. Nigel put his hands on his hips, watching intently. Ivy took his arm and turned him away.

"Hey, I was-"

"You came to save my life."

"Aye."

"You wore a ridiculous mask and hurt your hand."

"That I did."

"You saved the day. With some help."

"Now, listen-"

"Help you had the foresight to obtain."

"I'm no simpleton."

"My hero," Ivy said, taking Nigel's hand in hers.

***

"Ivy?! Have you seen my green jacket?"

Nigel groaned. He looked through the closet twice now, back to front, front to back, and it wasn't there.

"The forest green one?"

"No, the new one, that your mother purchased."

Ivy walked upstairs, carrying the coat on her arm. "This is olive green, darling," she said, holding it out.

Nigel took it and put it on. "I'm glad it doesn't smell like an olive."

Ivy smiled. "Are you ready?"

"For the most important day of my professional life? I may throw up something the color of this jacket."

Ivy wore a look of mock indignation on her face. "I believe in you and your passion for justice. You'll do fine."

Nigel took her in his arms, squeezing her tight. "Ivy Lovelace Barrington, I love you. I can't imagine getting through this life without you."

Ivy fought back tears. "I love you too."

They held the hug for a moment. Nigel let up and Ivy looked at him, a thoughtful pose on her face. "Would the theatrical 'break a leg' work this situation?"

"I sure hope not. Too many of them already. Best it be nothing more than muted social decorum mixed in with an errant fit of passion."

"Then let's hope for that."

Nigel started for the stairs.

"Just a moment," Ivy said.

He turned and faced her. She held a small gold shield in her hand. Gesturing him over, Ivy pinned it to his coat.

"Wouldn't do any good to forget your badge on your first day back on the job. And in court, no less."

***

When Nigel and Reginald arrived, the packed courthouse forced Reginald to stop when he saw the throng of gathered onlookers. Nigel had to take his arm and guide him inside.

"I see you don't take your own advice, good friend," Nigel said. "I was prepared for this."

"My word, look how many people there are. I didn't expect a crowd this size."

"I think they might hope to glimpse Her Majesty. After all, the Times quotes a source expressing the Queen's interest in this case."

"That's all I need," Reginald said.

"You're not the one going on the stand."

Once the trial of Chief Willoughby started, the Crown Prosecutor went over the evidence he would cover when he called Nigel to the stand. He would be one of many from the precinct that testified, and Nigel breezed through it.

Nigel spent the rest of the proceedings listening to details about the role that Willoughby was forced to play. He was no doubt duped by Rushforth and the like, but Nigel lamented the man's lack of courage, which could've saved him this trial and the likely sentence.

Nigel and Reginald sat by one another as the judge came in to pronounce the sentence. They rose, sharing an uneasy glance as the judge reminded the court of the charges. The sickly-looking man, face withered with time, pronounced Willoughby guilty, and ordered him to be hung.

His family cried out, prompting people to lead them out as Willoughby was taken away. Nigel gave his former boss credit, he didn't make a fuss or profess his innocence, he had a stoic look of resignation as they led him away.

Outside, Reginald waved to Nigel as he descended the steps.

"I didn't see that coming," Nigel said. "The culprits are dead. Why make an example?"

"The people needed a visual representation of justice."

"They had it. Those papers printed the death masks of Rushforth and his cronies."

"Not everyone can, or wants to, read the papers. This will provide closure; the Queen sets a hard line against murder and puts us all on notice."

"She could've just had a herald read a royal decree at the office."

Reginald smiled. Nigel hoped his friend would see his attempt to add levity and was glad he did.

The hanging took place later that night, to allow him a last meal with his family. Nigel and Reginald were there, near the front. He wore a suit, standing upright. His stare reminded Nigel of Willoughby delivering news of a murder to a victim's family. There was no joy in it, but you accepted the circumstance.

Willoughby's family sobbed as the former Chief was taken to the gallows.

"You will be alright," he said to them. "You will get through this."

His wife, thin, cried and managed a nod. The tears ran past her rouge and looked like blood.

Willoughby's gaze softened, and he risked a glance to the crowd. His eyes locked onto his former subordinates.

Nigel felt the blood drain from his face. He mustered a slight nod to his former superior, which he returned. If there was any ill will, Nigel didn't see it. *Maybe the nod was an apology. That's how I'll recall it.*

The pastor read to Willoughby as the hangmen placed the noose. Willoughby died moments later when the floor dropped out from under him.

***

Lord Ainsworth's trial as Rushforth's accomplice took place the next day, and Nigel dreaded having to go through the whole affair again. This time, he was lively and alert through the whole thing, because he felt Ainsworth was a pawn, and conveyed that in his testimony, emphasizing his continued cooperation with police and his help in finding the Barrington women.

To his surprise the court agreed. Instead of death, the crown stripped him of everything but his name and a few possessions. A portion of his estate paid for the burials of the deceased women. Nigel felt awful, buy Ivy told him to consider the alternative.

A jolt of surprise coursed through him when he spotted Ainsworth on his porch that morning, two days later. The young man wore one suit he could keep, his grooming impeccable.

"Lord Ainsworth, a fine surprise to see you here," Nigel said, then realized his words. "Please forgive me, I meant no offense. Habit, you see."

"None taken, Inspector. It'll be awhile before I am used to being called Hannibal, or lad, or god knows what."

"I'm sure. And please, you may call me Nigel, as soon as you tell me why you are here at this early hour."

"I start a position at Lovelace's today. He asked that I meet him here."

"I see," Nigel said, letting him in. "He failed to mention that to me."

"That's because he told me," Ivy said, standing in the hall. Minnie stood next to her, carrying a tray of tea and biscuits. "You had a lot on your plate this week, and I knew you didn't need the stress."

"That's mighty thoughtful of you." Nigel looked at Minnie, who stared at the young ex-noble. Ainsworth was equally smitten.

"Why don't we all go sit?" Ivy said, ignoring Nigel's inquisitive stare.

They sat and talked for twenty minutes, but it was mostly Ainsworth and Minnie chatting. Lovelace arrived to pick up Hannibal on his way to the office.

Nigel waved, closing the door. Minnie had already gone downstairs to help Charles with his invention.

"What was that about?"

"I told you."

"Did your father really invite him over here?"

"Are you calling me a liar, Inspector?"

"I'm calling you a sneaky matchmaker."

Ivy smiled. "I merely bring people together who should be."

Nigel groaned as he grabbed his coat, as Ivy laughed. "I'm off to keep you safe. Might have to send someone over, monitor you and my sister."

***

Nigel walked in to the Inspector's office, where Reginald pored over paperwork. "Nothing like a crime scene, eh?"

"Beats looking at blood and mutilated bodies. Thanks for coming in early."

"I hope you will not evoke friendship favors and make this a habit."

"This will be it, I promise. I need something. My predecessor deemed it unnecessary to have an Assistant Chief. I do not know why, but there is no way I'll survive without it.

You've stood by my side since we started here, Nigel. I wouldn't want anyone else next to me as long as I'm here."

"I'm flattered, and as long as this isn't a habit, I accept."

Reginald stood and shook his hand. "That's a relief. I didn't need additional difficulties my first day."

Michael knocked on the door and saluted before entering. "Forgive me, sir, but there's a robbery in progress at the Covington Mill. They request our assistance."

Reginald threw the paper down. "I thought you'd never ask," he said, then looked at Nigel. "You with me?"

"Always."

Nigel followed Reginald to the cab, looking around at the city of London. He smiled. His home was in excellent hands with Reginald at the helm, and Nigel got back to a job he loved. Nigel entered the cab, eager to do his part to keep London safe.

SIX MONTHS LATER

igel ran from the cab to Lovelace Industries headquarters. The clerk, a boy of sixteen, waved as he entered.

"Is Mr. Lovelace here?"

"No, sir. He went with your brother to tout Charles's contraption to investors."

"And Mr. Ainsworth?"

"In his office, sir."

Nigel and ran to the far corner of the factory floor. There, Hannibal Ainsworth bit into bread, huddled over financial records. He wore an apron over his clothes. He told Nigel over dinner he oversaw making production more efficient, besides monitoring the finances of Lovelace Industries.

Hannibal smiled when he saw Nigel. "Good morning. Minnie isn't here today, nor is Charles."

Ainsworth announced his intention to marry Minnie a month ago, and negotiations between Nigel and Hannibal concluded over dinner three nights prior.

Nigel couldn't help but feel a profound sense of gratitude towards Ainsworth for his commitment to watching over Charles.

He wouldn't say it aloud just yet, but it thrilled Nigel to have the young man join the family.

"I'm here to see you. I'm sure you've heard the news report of sightings of a beast?"

Ainsworth laughed. "Interesting notions to be sure."

"They're real. Only it's not a beast, but a man augmented with a potion of some kind. I need your help to apprehend him."

"I'm not sure what I can do."

"It has come to my attention that your...evening ensemble was never turned over to evidence."

Ainsworth swallowed hard. "Listen, Nigel, I-"

"Do you still have it?"

A heartbeat's pause. "Yes."

"Good. Want to use it, and help me save London?"

Ainsworth smiled.

ACKNOWLEDGEMENTS

No man is an island, certainly not one who wants to publish a novel. Thank you to Steve Bays, Rebecca Owens and Walt Stoffel for being my beta readers. Kayinat Kashif, your editing was invaluable. Thank you for helping me make this the best it can be.

Thank you to Boundless Book Design for consulting on the cover.

I have to give a special shout out to author K.W. Jeter, who coined the word steampunk all the way back in 1987. It would be another fifteen years before I discovered this genre and I was hooked from the get-go. Thank you to the writers, artists – on Deviantart.com, Pinterest and other outlets that have inspired my imagination since.

My kids, Dylon and Breanna, you're my best creation. I love you and I'm so proud of you both.

Michelle, your love and support mean the world to me. I love sharing this life with you.

Finally, thank you to everyone to who supports independent authors. You mean the world to us.

THANK YOU so much for reading *The Petticoat Society*! If you enjoyed this book, I would be so honored if you would please take a few moments to write a review of it. You can do that by going to https://tinyurl.com/TPSAZreview or using the QR code below.

Keep reading for a sneak peak of the next adventure in the Tales of Gears & Grit, *Aeronauts!*

— · —

1

Catherine Pemberton couldn't hide her smile as she sat down for the lunch that would spell her end. Her new dress fit perfectly, even with the corset clamping down on her innards. Aunt Evelyn pulled it so tight, it took her a few deep breaths to stop feeling like she was suffocating.

"Perfect for posture, my dear," Evelyn had said, her nasally, high-pitched voice adding to Catherine's discomfort. "You cannot expect to win a husband if you cannot even sit up straight."

She put that thought behind her as she walked by her aunt, slowing down to keep pace as they traversed London's streets. It would not do to walk in front of her chaperone, who was on strict orders from Catherine's father, Lieutenant Pemberton, to observe decorum to the letter, at all times, or Evelyn was within her right to bring her brother's daughter home and end her courtship.

Catherine did manage to convince her father to bring a parasol. Despite it not being overly hot on this early May afternoon, she told her father that her attempts to concentrate on following the rules might make her overheat, and causing a scene wouldn't make a good look for her or the family and the Lieutenant agreed.

She smiled at the thought, because she could use the parasol to signal her intentions to her beloved, something that Evelyn never did, and Catherine had found ignorant of its use.

This mostly forgotten accessory was the most important piece of the evening, at least to Catherine. She begrudgingly let her Aunt and father dictate her ensemble. That didn't matter. She was already aware of Roderick Caine's fondness for her, but they had been courting now for nearly a year, and she knew that he had met with her father on at least two occasions, but he was parsimonious with details. But if he would risk her father's generous ire, then things were as serious as Catherine had hoped. The parasol would tell all.

According to general rules of decorum in these matters - and they always changed, but she confirmed with her cousin, Mildred, that they were still current, dropping the parasol would require an answer of her suitor - did he love her? Catherine had no doubts, and with tonight's stunt, she would confirm it, and put pressure on her father, through his sister, Evelyn, to get this engagement done.

She was incensed that her neighbor, Clara, was almost two years her junior and was already engaged six months into a courtship. And that girl didn't have the resources that the Lieutenant did for a dowry. Given his standing in Her Majesty's Navy, and designs on advancement, father expressed his desire for Catherine to marry. But the war was over, and father fully recovered from his injuries. What was the issue?

The server brought over tea and biscuits, the buttery coating reflecting off the sun coming in from the windows. Catherine didn't realize she was hungry until then, and reached for one. Evelyn cleared her throat, and a stern look on her face reminded Catherine she had to wait.

"Get used to it, dear," Evelyn said, taking a biscuit. She gestured to Catherine and eyed the teapot. Catherine lifted it, the spout titled toward her Aunt. Evelyn made a small noise, and Catherine pulled it back, taking a breath.

The proper handling and pouring of tea is a pre-cursor to your duty as a wife. Evelyn told her that at least once a week, and she heard that in her head now. Adjusting her grip, she poured the perfect cup of tea, which her aunt acknowledged with curt nod.

"Now," Evelyn started, only to look past Catherine.

"Please forgive me tardiness, Miss Pemberton," a strong, yet soft baritone voice said behind them. Catherine turned and smiled as she laid eyes on a six foot tall man with trimmed mustache. He filled in his dark plaid suit nicely, and his ice blue eyes could get one lost in there. He removed his bowler hat, his brown hair perfectly coiffed. He bowed and kissed her hand.

"That's quite all right, Mr. Caine," Catherine said, almost out of breath as she did so. He had that power over her. Catherine sure hoped that Evelyn was ignorant of this notion.

To make sure her Aunt remained that way, Catherine moved to compose herself. Whether by fortuitous luck, or by her beloved recognizing her needs at this moment, Roderick stepped between her and her aunt, affording her time to catch her breath and calm her breathing - a task that took longer than normal due to the corset.

Roderick took a bit more time than decorum required to greet Evelyn, so Catherine was herself again when he stood. He truly is the man God sent for me.

"Please join us," Evelyn said, gesturing for him to take the seat between them. Catherine was pleased that they were given a square table, so that Roderick could be next to her. She made sure, upon sitting, that she had plenty of room to her right so that she could rub her foot against Roderick's leg. Scandalous, for sure, but this wouldn't be the first time they acted in a such a manner.

'Discretion affords us many benefits,' Roderick had told her with a wink and that smile she had come to love. That saying stuck with her during their entire courtship to date, and she had no doubt it would serve her well in the future.

"You said something about airships?" Catherine asked, pouring Roderick tea. She didn't look at Evelyn, but still felt her gaze as she lifted it and poured him a cup. This time, it was perfect, because the corners of her aunt's mouth curved upwards.

"Indeed," Roderick said, taking two sugar cubes for her tea. Evelyn's left arm twitched. It was subtle, as if she wanted to reach for something but decided against it. He didn't see it. Anyone else would have just thought it a nervous tic, but Catherine knew better. Evelyn disapproved of two cubes of sugar? It seemed trifle, but anything that could negatively affect her engagement would need to be countered, no matter how insignificant. Catherine filed that away to ask Evelyn about on the walk home.

"It's most peculiar," he said, taking a sip of tea. "My brother, the younger one in the Royal Air Corps, didn't mention aerial exercises. He is most keen on getting up in the sky."

Catherine listened intently, gripping the parasol in her hand. She felt her heart beating faster, hammering against her chest - accentuated by the corset. Catherine had to time her releasing of the parasol correctly, so as to not arouse suspicion in her aunt. Fortunately, she had practiced many times over tea with her cousin, so she felt she had it all figured out.

"I can't imagine her Majesty is allowing more of them to crowd the skies," Roderick continued, taking a biscuit and buttering it. He took a bite, moaning softly. Catherine looked down to suppress her smile. He made the sound once before, when she nibbled on his ear.

"But we are a growing Empire, and progress stops for no one," he said, winking at Catherine as he drank some more tea. He put it down and Catherine saw his eyes lock onto the ham.

This is it!

"Would you care for some jam, Mr. Caine?" She asked.

He lifted his hand toward it, but immediately dropped it. "That would be lovely."

Catherine held her breath, and reached for it with her left land, dropping the parasol at the same time. "Oh my," she cried out, trying to add an extra layer of shock into her voice.

She bent down to pick it, but not as fast as Evelyn, or anyone paying attention, would have expected. She heard murmurs go up around her, and people slide their chairs back. Was that this much of a faux pas?

Bending down as far as she could - that damn corset and its restrictions - she waited a moment. The perfectly polished boots of her beloved were in front of her. She counted four heartbeats, waiting for him to join her and give his answer.

Instead, his chair moved back, and those boots with it. Catherine gasped. Was this his answer? Did her action repulse him?

The tears welled up in her seconds later, much worse than when she over-served tea to her mother the first time.

A loud bang filled the air, and for a moment, she thought it was her heart leaping out of her chest. Roderick's whisper of "My word" made her sick to her stomach. No, no, no, this isn't supposed to happen!

Had she misjudged him? She couldn't have. Evelyn was here and providing her father with reports. He kept warning her or decorum and the family name. One doesn't do that if there is no courtship.

And those nights in the park, when they snuck away from Evelyn....

Catherine heard a whimper escape her mouth, but steeled herself. There would be no tears. She wasn't one of these helpless waifs who needed a man to survive. She wanted love. And if Roderick didn't feel love for her, then she would make him say it.

She sat up, her eyes boring into her suitor. They softened when she saw his, big as saucers, his jaw opened. He was focused on the window to the left.

The last thing she felt was not the summer heat of London, but the engulfing flames of the bomb that exploded behind her.

ABOUT THE AUTHOR

Jason Prugar is an award-winning short filmmaker, novelist, and short story writer. He enjoys playing sports, watching films and spending time with his family. He lives with his partner, children, and three dogs in Pennsylvania.

www.ingramcontent.com/pod-product-compliance
Lightning Source LLC
Chambersburg PA
CBHW070508160726
48003CB00004B/1476